# DEBBIE MACOMBER

## *Starry Night*

arrow books

Published by Arrow Books 2013

4 6 8 10 9 7 5

First published in Great Britain in 2013 by
Arrow Books
Random House, 20 Vauxhall Bridge Road,
London SW1V 2SA

www.randomhouse.co.uk

Addresses for companies within The Random House Group Limited can be
found at: www.randomhouse.co.uk/offices.htm

The Random House Group Limited Reg. No. 954009

A CIP catalogue record for this book
is available from the British Library

ISBN 9780099564126

The Random House Group Limited supports the Forest Stewardship
Council® (FSC®), the leading international forest-certification organisation.
Our books carrying the FSC label are printed on FSC®-certified paper. FSC is
the only forest-certification scheme supported by the leading environmental
organisations, including Greenpeace. Our paper procurement policy can
be found at: www.randomhouse.co.uk/environment

Typeset by SX Composing DTP, Rayleigh, Essex
Printed in Great Britain by Clays Ltd, St Ives plc

To Conny and Gina Johannesson
in appreciation of your
friendship and talent

Christmas 2013

Dear Friends,

As you might have already guessed, I'm one of those Christmas fanatics. Christmas trees, nativity scenes, lights, and a multitude of decorations fill our home and yard from Thanksgiving through New Year's. Because of my love for the season, I've written a Christmas story each year simply because I couldn't allow the holidays to pass without putting my own unique stamp on them.

Many of my readers tell me they started reading my books after picking up one of my Christmas stories. Over the years I've penned tales involving angelic beings— Shirley, Goodness, and Mercy—and I wouldn't dare forget to add Mrs. Miracle, one of your favorites and mine, too. Then there were the romantic comedies, some of which I wrote with tears in my eyes from laughing so hard.

*Starry Night* is a bit of a departure for me. It's a romance, plain and simple. An absolutely wildly romantic tale involving one of my favorite spots on this green earth— Alaska. I've flown above the Arctic Circle myself with my husband, Wayne, and viewed the northern lights. Some of you might recognize Sawyer O'Halloran, who makes an appearance just for fun, from my Midnight Sons series.

I'm blessed to work with one of the most incredible teams in publishing. Shauna Summers and Jennifer Hershey edited this story. Theresa Park, my agent, has been my most ardent cheerleader, along with Rachel Bressler. The Random House crew—Libby McGuire, Susan Corcoran, Kim Hovey, and Kristin Fassler—has added its magic touches as well in making sure this story, and all my books, gets the most exposure possible. And that, my friends, is only the tip of the iceberg. My own staff—Renate Roth, Heidi Pollard, Carol Bass, Wanda Roberts, Adele LaCombe, and Katie Rouner—has become both my right and my left hand. To each one I owe a huge note of appreciation.

While I'm eager to fill in details of the story, I refuse to deny you the pleasure of sitting back, turning the pages, and digging in. And when you finish, my hope is that you will close the book, sigh, and claim this is one of my most romantic Christmas stories you've ever read.

Merry Christmas!

*Debbie Macomber*

P.S. I always enjoy hearing from my readers.
You can reach me through Facebook or my website at www.debbiemacomber.com or at P.O. Box 1458, Port Orchard, WA 98366.

# Starry Night

# Chapter 1

Carrie Slayton's feet were killing her. She'd spent the last ninety minutes standing in two-inch heels at a charity art auction in a swanky studio in downtown Chicago. She couldn't understand how shoes that matched her black dress so beautifully could be this painful. Vanity, thy name is fashion.

"My name is spelled with two *l*s," the middle-aged woman, dripping in diamonds, reminded her. "That's Michelle, with two *l*s."

"Got it." Carrie underlined the correct spelling. Michelle, spelled with two *l*s, had just spent thirty thousand dollars for the most ridiculous piece of art Carrie had ever seen. True, it was for a good cause, but now she seemed to feel her name needed to be mentioned in the news article Carrie would write for the next edition of the *Chicago Herald*.

"It would be wonderful to have my husband's and my picture to go along with your article," Michelle added. "Perhaps you should take it in front of the painting."

Carrie looked over her shoulder at Harry, the photographer who'd accompanied her from the newspaper.

"Of course, Lloyd and I would want approval of any photograph you choose to publish."

"Of course," Carrie said, doing her best to keep a smile in place. If she didn't get out of these shoes soon, her feet would be permanently deformed. She wiggled her toes, hoping for relief. Instead they ached even worse.

Harry, bless his heart, dutifully stepped forward, camera in hand, and flashed two or three photos of the couple posing in front of what might have been a red flower or a painting of a squished tomato or possibly the aftermath of a murder scene. Carrie had yet to decide which. The title of the work didn't offer a clue. *Red*. Yes, the painting was in that color, but exactly what it depicted remained a mystery.

"Isn't it stunning?" Michelle asked when she noticed Carrie staring at the canvas.

Carrie tilted her head one way and then another,

looking for some clue as to its possible significance. Then, noticing that Michelle, spelled with two *l*'s, was waiting for her response, she said, "Oh, yes, it's amazing."

Harry didn't bother to hide his smile, knowing that all Carrie really wanted was to get out of those ridiculous shoes. And to think she'd gotten her journalism degree for this!

Carrie knew she was fortunate to have a job with such a prestigious newspaper. A professor had pulled a favor and gotten her the interview. Carrie had been stunned when she'd been hired. Surprised and overjoyed.

Two years later, she was less so. Her assignment was the society page. When she was hired, she'd been told that eventually she'd be able to write meatier pieces, do interviews and human-interest stories. To this point, it hadn't happened. Carrie felt trapped, frustrated, and underappreciated. She felt her talent was being wasted.

To make matters worse, her entire family lived in the Pacific Northwest. Carrie had left everything she knew and loved behind, including Steve, her college sweetheart. He'd married less than six months after she took the position in Chicago. It hadn't taken him long, she noted. The worst part was that Carrie was far too busy reporting on social events to have time for much of a social life herself. She dated occasionally, but she hadn't found anyone who made her heart race. Dave Schneider, the man she'd been seeing most recently, was more of a friend than a love interest. She supposed after Steve she was a bit hesitant to get involved again. Maybe once she left the *Herald* and moved home to write for a newspaper in the Seattle area, like she planned, things would be different.

Back inside her condo, Carrie gingerly removed her shoes and sighed with relief.

This was it. She was done. First thing in the morning she would hand in her two-week notice, sublet her condo, and take her chances in the job market in Seattle. If the managing editor, Nash Jorgen, refused to give her the opportunity to prove she had what it took, then why stay? She refused to be pigeonholed.

That decided, Carrie limped into her bedroom and fell into bed, tired, frustrated, and determined to make a change.

"You can't be serious," argued Sophie Peterson, her closest friend at the newspaper, when Carrie told her of her decision.

"I'm totally serious," she said as she hobbled to her desk.

"What's wrong with your foot?" Sophie asked, tagging behind her.

"Stupidity. This gorgeous pair of shoes was only available in a half-size smaller than what I normally wear. They were so perfect, and they were buy one pair, get the second half off. I couldn't resist, but now I'm paying for it."

"Carrie, don't do it."

"Don't worry, I have no intention of wearing those heels again. I tossed them in a bag for charity."

"Not that," Sophie argued. "Don't hand in your notice! You're needed here."

"Not as a reporter," Carrie assured her, dumping her purse in her bottom drawer and shucking off her thick winter coat. "Sorry, my mind is made up. You and I both know Nash will never give me a decent assignment."

"You're your own worst enemy." Sophie leaned against the wall that separated their two cubicles and crossed her arms and ankles.

"How's that?"

"Well, for one thing, you're the perfect fit for the society page. You're drop-dead gorgeous, tall, and thin. It doesn't hurt that you look fabulous in a slinky black dress and a pair of spike heels. Even if I could get my hair to grow that thick, long, and curly without perming the living daylights out of it, Nash would never consider someone like me. It isn't any wonder he wants you on the job. Give the guy a little credit, will you? He knows what he's doing."

"If looks are the only criterion—"

"There's more," Sophie said, cutting her off. "You're great with people. All you need to do is bat those baby blues at them and strangers open up to you. It's a gift, I tell you, a real gift."

"Okay, I'm friendly, but this isn't the kind of writing I want to do. I've got my heart set on being a reporter, a real reporter, writing about real news and interesting people." In the beginning, Carrie had been flattered by the way people went out of their way to introduce themselves at the events she covered. It didn't take long for her to recognize that they were looking for her to mention their names in print. What shocked her was the extent people were willing to go in order to be noticed. She was quickly becoming jaded, and this bothered her even more than Nash's lack of faith in her abilities.

The holidays were the worst, and while it was only early November, the frenzy had already started. The list of parties Nash assigned her to attend was already mammoth. Halloween decorations were still arranged around her desk, and already there was a Christmas tree in the display window of the department store across the street.

Determined to stick with her plan, Carrie went directly into Nash Jorgen's office.

A veteran newsman, Nash glanced up from his computer screen and glared in her direction. He seemed to sense this wasn't a social visit. His shoulders rose with a weary sigh. "What now?" he growled.

"I'm handing in my two-week notice." If she'd been looking for a response, she would have been disappointed.

He blinked a couple of times, ran his hand down the side of his day-old beard, and asked, "Any particular reason?"

"I hoped to prove I can be a darn good reporter, but I'll never get the chance writing anything more than copy for society weddings. You said when you hired me that you'd give me a shot at reporting real news."

"I don't remember what I said. What's wrong with what you're writing now? You're good."

"It isn't what I want to write."

"So? You make the best of it, pay your dues, and in time you'll get the break you're looking for."

Carrie was tired of waiting. She straightened her

shoulders, her resolve tightening. "I know I'm fortunate to work for the *Herald*. It was a real coup to get this position, but this isn't the career I wanted. You give me no choice." She set her letter of resignation on his desk.

That got Nash's attention. He swiveled his chair around to look at her once more. His frown darkened, and he ran his hand through his thinning hair. "You really are serious, aren't you?"

A chill went down her spine. Nash was actually listening. "Yes, I'm serious."

"Fine, then." He reached across his desk and picked up a hardcover book and handed it to her. "Find Finn Dalton, get an interview, and write me a story I can print."

She grabbed hold of the book, not recognizing the author's name. "And if I do?"

"Well, first, there's a snowball's chance of you even locating him. Every reporter in the universe is dying to interview him. But if you get lucky and he's willing to talk and we print the piece, then I'll take you off the society page."

Carrie wavered. He seemed to be offering her a chance, as impossible as it might seem. Now it was up to her to prove herself. She dared not show him how excited she was. "I'll find him."

He snickered as though he found her confidence amusing, and then sobered. He regarded her with the same dark frown he had earlier before a slow, easy smile slid over his harsh features. "I bet you will. Now, listen up—if you get an interview with Finn Dalton, you can have any assignment you want."

Taking small steps, Carrie backed out of the office. She pointed at Nash. "I'm holding you to your word."

The managing editor was already back to reading his computer screen and didn't appear to have heard her. It didn't matter; she'd heard him, and he'd come across loud and clear.

Once she was out of his office, she examined the book to see the author photo, but couldn't find one, not even on the inside back flap.

Walking back to her cubicle, she paused at Sophie's instead. "You ever heard of Finn Dalton?"

Sophie's eyebrows lifted on her round face. "You mean you haven't?"

"No." The book title wasn't much help. *Alone.* That told her next to nothing. The jacket revealed a snow-covered landscape with a scattering of stubby trees.

Sophie shook her head. "Have you been living under a rock?"

"No. Who is this guy?"

"He's a survivalist who lives alone someplace in the Alaskan wilderness."

"Oh." That was a bit daunting, but Carrie considered herself up to the challenge. She'd been born and raised in Washington State. She'd hoped to join her family for Thanksgiving, but if she needed to use her vacation time to find Finn Dalton, then she was willing to.

"His book has been on the bestseller lists for nearly seven months, mostly at the number-one position."

Carrie was impressed. "What does he write about?"

"He's the kind of guy you can set loose in the wild with a pack of chewing gum, a pocketknife, and a handkerchief, and by the time you find him he's built a shelter and a canoe. From what I've read, his stories about Alaskan life and survival in the tundra would kink your hair. Well, not that yours needs curling."

This was Sophie's idea of a joke. Carrie's wild dark brown curls were the bane of her existence. She tamed them as best she could, but she often found herself the brunt of jokes over her out-of-control hair.

"Nash says he doesn't give interviews."

"Not just doesn't give interviews—this guy is like a ghost. No one has ever met or even talked to him."

"Surely his publisher or his editor—"

"No," Sophie said, cutting her off. "Everything has been done by computer."

"Well, then . . ."

"All anyone knows is that he lives near an Alaskan lake somewhere in the vicinity of the Arctic Circle."

"How is it you know so much about this guy?"

"I don't, and that's just it. No one does. The press has gone wild looking for him. Plenty of reporters have tried to track him down, without success. No one knows how to find him, and Finn Dalton doesn't want to be found. He should have called his book *Leave Me Alone*. Someone could pass him on the street and never know it was him, and from everything I've read, that's exactly how he likes it."

Intrigued, Carrie flipped through the pages of the book. "Nash said I could have any assignment I wanted if I got an interview from Finn Dalton."

"Of course he did. Nash has been around long enough to know he's got you in a no-win situation."

Carrie glanced up. "I don't care. I'm going to try."

"I hate to be a killjoy here, but Carrie, no way will you find this guy. Better reporters than either of us have tried and failed. Every newspaper, magazine, and media outlet is looking to dig up information about him, without success. Finn Dalton doesn't want to be found."

That might be the case, but Carrie refused to give up without even trying. This was far too important to drop just because it was a long shot. "I'm desperate, Sophie." And really, that said it all. If she was going to have a real career in journalism, she had to find Finn Dalton. Her entire future with the *Chicago Herald* hung in the balance.

"I admire your determination," Sophie murmured, "but I'm afraid you're going to hit one dead end after another."

"That might be the case." Carrie was willing to admit to her friend that finding Finn Dalton wouldn't be easy. "But I refuse to quit without trying." She knew Sophie didn't mean to be negative. "I want this chance, and if it means tracking Finn Dalton into some forsaken tundra, then I will put on my big-girl shoes and go for it." But not the heels she'd worn last night, that was for sure.

The first thing Carrie did in her search for Finn Dalton was read the book. Not once, but three times. She underlined everything that gave her a single hint as to his identity.

For two days she skipped lunch, spending her time on the computer, seeking any bit of information she could find that would help her locate Finn Dalton. She went from one search engine to another.

"How's it going?" Sophie asked as they met each other on their way out the door a couple of days later.

"Good." Through her fact-finding mission, Carrie was getting a picture of the man who had written this amazing book. After a third read she almost felt as if she knew him. He hadn't always been a recluse. He'd been raised in Alaska and had learned to live off the land from his father, whom he apparently idolized. One thing was certain, he seemed to have no use for women. In the entire book, not once did he mention his mother or any other female influence. It was more of what he didn't say that caught Carrie's attention.

"Any luck?" Sophie asked, breaking into her thoughts.

"Not yet." She hesitated. "Have you read the book?"

Sophie nodded. "Sure. Nearly everyone has."

"Did you notice he has nothing to say about the opposite sex? I have the feeling he distrusts women."

Sophie shrugged as if she hadn't paid much notice, but then she hadn't been reading between the lines the way Carrie had.

"How old do you think he is?" Sophie asked.

"I can't really say." Finn was an excellent writer and storyteller. But the tales he relayed could have happened at nearly any point in the last several decades. Current events were skipped over completely.

Sophie crossed her arms and looked thoughtful. "My guess is that he's fifty or so, to have survived on his own all these years."

Speculation wouldn't do Carrie any good. "Tell you what. When I find out, you'll be the first to know. Deal?"

Sophie smiled and nodded. "Deal."

That night, as Carrie readied for her latest charity event, her cell rang. It was her mother in Seattle. They spoke at least two or three times a week. Carrie was tight with her family and missed them dreadfully.

"Hi, Mom," she answered, pressing her cell to one ear while she attempted to place a pearl earring in her other earlobe.

"Hi, sweetheart. Are you busy?"

"I've got a couple of minutes." She switched ears and stabbed the second pearl into place before tucking her feet into a comfortable pair of high heels. She was scheduled to meet Harry in thirty minutes.

"Dad and I are so excited to see you at Thanksgiving."

"Yes, about that." Carrie grabbed her purse and tucked it under her arm while holding on to her phone.

"Mom, I hate to tell you this, but there's a possibility I might not make it home for Thanksgiving."

"What?"

The disappointment in her mother's voice was painful to hear. "Have you ever heard of Finn Dalton?"

"Oh, sure. Your father loved his book so much he bought two additional copies. I read it, too. Now, that's a man."

"I want to interview him."

"Really? From what I understand, he doesn't give interviews."

"Yeah, that's what I heard, too."

"Does he ever come to Chicago?"

"Doubtful," Carrie murmured. If only it could be that easy and he would come to her. Well, that wasn't likely. Then again, something Sophie said had stayed in her mind. She could walk past him on the sidewalk and never know it was him. "I'll need to track Finn Dalton down, but I keep running into dead ends the same as everyone else." She mentioned her online search, the calls to Alaska, and the number of phones slammed in her ear. No one had been willing to talk to her. "I have to look at this from a different angle. Have you got any ideas?"

"From what your father said, Finn Dalton isn't a man who would enjoy being written up on the society page."

"That's just it, Mom. This would be an investigative piece. My editor told me I could have my pick of assignments if I was able to get this interview. It's important, enough for me to take the vacation days I planned to use for Thanksgiving to find him."

"Oh, Carrie, I hate the thought of you doing that."

"I know, I hate it, too, but it's necessary." Her mother was well aware of Carrie's feelings toward her current work situation.

"Do you really think you can find Finn Dalton?" her mother asked.

"I don't know if I can or not, but if I don't, it won't be for lack of trying."

"I've always admired your tenacious spirit. Can I tell your father you're going to write a piece on the man who wrote *Alone*?"

"Ah . . . not yet. I have to locate Dalton first."

"What have you discovered so far?" Her mother was nothing if not practical. Carrie could visualize her mother pushing up her shirtsleeves, ready to tackle this project with Carrie.

"Do you know where he was born?"

"No. I assumed it must have been Alaska, but there's no record of his birth there. I've started going through the birth records of other states, starting with the northwest, but haven't found his name yet." At this rate, it would be the turn of the next century before she found the right Dalton.

"What about his schooling? Graduation records?"

"I tried that, but he's not listed anywhere. Maybe he was homeschooled."

"You're probably right," her mother said, sounding proud that Carrie had reasoned it out. "One of his stories mentions his father mailing away for books, remember? Those were textbooks, I bet."

Carrie had made the same assumption.

"Finn is a rather unusual name, isn't it?" her mother continued softly, as though she was thinking out loud.

"And of course it could be a pseudonym, but his publisher claims the name is as real as the man." Nothing seemed the norm when it came to Finn Dalton.

"You know, work on the Alaskan pipeline was very big about the time your father and I got married. That was a huge project, and it brought a lot of men to Alaska; many of them stayed. His father might have been one of them."

"Yes." But that was a stab in the dark. She'd already spent hours going over every type of record she could think to research from Alaska, to no avail. Carrie glanced at the time, even though this talk was helping her generate ideas of where to continue looking for the mysterious Mr. Dalton.

"From what I remember, a lot of men left their wives and families for the attraction of big money."

"I could start looking at the employment records for the pipeline from that time period and see what I find," Carrie said.

"That's a terrific idea. And listen, when you find Finn Dalton, make sure your dad gets a chance to chat with him, would you?"

"I can't promise that." First she'd need to convince Finn Dalton to talk to her!

"Just do your best."

"I'll do what I can."

"Bye, sweetie."

"Bye, Mom." Carrie ended the call and dumped her cell in her small bag. After a quick glance in the hallway mirror, she headed out the door to what she hoped would be one of the very last social events she would ever need to cover.

# Chapter 2

This had to be Finn Dalton's mother. It simply had to be. From the moment Nash had given Carrie what seemed like the impossible assignment of interviewing Finn, she'd looked for out-of-the-box ways to locate him. Her mother's mention of work on the Alaskan pipeline and that many of those employed came from Washington State had led to a breakthrough. At least she hoped so. The search led Carrie to the birth record for a Finnegan Paul Dalton, not in Alaska but in her own birth state of Washington. That record revealed his mother's name—Joan Finnegan Dalton—which then led to a divorce decree, along with a license for a second marriage several years later. Tax records indicated that Joan, whose married name was now Reese, continued to reside in Washington State. Her hope was that Joan Dalton Reese would be willing to help Carrie find Finn.

The November wind and rain whipped against her as she walked up the short pathway to the single-family house in Kent, a suburb south of Seattle.

Nerves made Carrie tense as she rang the doorbell and waited. After a few moments, she heard footsteps on the other side of the door. The woman who opened it didn't look to be much older than her own mother.

"Joan Finnegan Dalton Reese?" Carrie asked.

The petite, dark-haired woman blinked warily, and her eyes widened as if she wasn't sure what to think. "Yes?"

"By chance are you related to Finnegan Paul Dalton?"

She didn't answer right away, and then her gaze narrowed. "You're another one of those reporters, aren't you?"

"Yes, I—"

Joan started to close the door, but Carrie quickly inserted her foot, stopping her.

The two women stared hard at each other. "Yes, I'm a reporter, but I'm hoping you'll hear me out."

"Why should I?" she demanded, and crossed her arms over her chest.

Carrie frantically searched for something that would convince the other woman to talk to her. "I can't think of a single reason other than the fact that I'm tired of writing for the society page. I gave up spending time with my family over Thanksgiving with the hope that I could get this interview, and I think you have an incredible son, and I'd very much like to meet and interview him."

The delicate woman looked undecided. "What do you mean you write for the society page?"

Carrie explained how she'd taken a few of her precious vacation days and flown to Seattle. It'd been a risk, but one she was willing to take. This would be the first year she'd missed the holiday with her parents, aunts, uncles, and cousins. Although it would be a sacrifice, her parents understood that if she did manage to interview Finn Dalton, then she would have her pick of writing assignments, and not just in Chicago, but perhaps in the Pacific Northwest. "I want to move back to Seattle to be closer to my family, and this is my chance."

Joan eyed her carefully, and then, after what seemed like an eternity, she slowly opened the door, silently inviting Carrie inside.

"Thank you," she whispered. "Thank you so much." Stepping out of the cold, Carrie instantly felt the warm flow of air surround her. She noticed a bronze pumpkin off to the right and a doll-sized set of pilgrims on the dining room table.

Joan motioned toward the living room. "How much do you know about my son?"

Carrie sat on the edge of the sofa cushion, unsure how best to answer. She could attempt to bluff or she could be direct in the hope that Joan Reese would be willing to help her. "Well, only what I've read in his book and what I've learned online, which isn't much."

"Unfortunately, I don't know how much help I'll be. I haven't talked to my Finn in five years, not since his father died . . . he told me he wants nothing more to do with me."

Carrie read the pain in the other woman's eyes, and not knowing how to react, she leaned forward and placed her hand on Joan's forearm.

"I tried to connect with him after his father's death, but Finn made it clear that I had nothing to say that he wanted to hear." She wadded a tissue in her hands and kept her head lowered.

"So you don't have any idea where Finn is living?"

Carrie asked, her heart thumping with hope and expectation.

"Alaska, somewhere outside Fairbanks, but then you probably already know that."

Seeing that he'd written extensively about life in the frozen north, this was the one piece of information she did have. And apparently so did every other news agency. His book told of adventures on the tundra, which indicated his cabin was most likely situated near the Arctic Circle. And that meant the only way to reach him would be by air, which would involve hiring a bush pilot.

"I've tried to find someone in Alaska to help me"—Carrie explained her efforts to talk to a number of resources, including bush pilots—"but it's been one dead end after another."

"At least you're honest about being a reporter," Joan said. "You couldn't imagine what some of them have tried, thinking I could give them information that would lead them to my son. You, at least, are willing to admit why you're doing this."

"He probably never suspected this interest in him and his lifestyle would happen. People love his stories, and now they want to know about the man behind them."

"He never forgave me, you see . . ." Joan murmured, her voice trailing away as she methodically tore apart the tissue in her hands.

"Forgave you?"

"I left him and his father when Finn was a boy. Paul loved Alaska, and I was born in Louisiana. I tried to make a life with him up there, but I couldn't bear the cold and the isolation, whereas Paul and Finn seemed to thrive on it. I wanted us to compromise, come back to the lower forty-eight a few months each year, but Paul wasn't willing to consider that. He insisted there was nothing for him outside Alaska. He felt any time away would be a waste. He had a dozen different projects going all the time and refused to leave. I wanted Finn to come with me, but my son chose to stay with his father." She paused and looked away as if she regretted having spoken. "Once I left, Paul cut me completely out of his life, and Finn's, too. Eventually I remarried, but it was more for companionship than love. Finn never forgave me for that, either. I think he must have held on to the dream that his father and I would reunite one day. My second husband died a year ago, so I'm a widow twice over."

"I'm so sorry," Carrie said.

"I wish I knew the man Finn has become," Joan whispered.

"If I find him and have a chance to talk to him, I'll tell him about meeting you. I can give him a message from you, even if it's just to remind him that you love him and want to hear from him."

Joan glanced up and her eyes brightened with what could be described only as ragged hope. "You'd do that?"

"Of course." As close as she was to her own family, Carrie's heart went out to Finn's mother, still looking to connect with her son. Although she didn't know him beyond the pages of his book, she couldn't help wonder about a man who would turn his back on his mother.

"Then perhaps there's a small way I can help," Joan said, her eyes twinkling now.

"There is?" She had Carrie's full attention.

Joan left the room and returned a few moments later with a simple gold ring. "This was Paul's wedding band. When we divorced . . . he was angry and bitter, and he returned the ring to me. I've saved it all these years, and now that Paul is dead I would like Finn to have it."

"You want me to give Finn his father's ring?"

Joan nodded. "Finn has a friend named Sawyer. He's a bush pilot who is often in Fairbanks. I could see Sawyer felt bad for the way Finn spoke to me at his father's funeral, and I think he might be willing to help you find my son if you give him a good enough reason."

Carrie smiled and held the gold band between her index finger and thumb. This ring could very well be her ticket to reaching the elusive Finn Dalton.

"You found him?" Sophie shouted from the other end of the cell phone. "You actually found Finn Dalton?"

Carrie meandered through the Fairbanks airport, dragging her carry-on behind her with one hand and holding the cell phone to her ear with the other. Her high-heeled boots made tapping sounds against the floor as she left the baggage-claim area. "I haven't found him yet," Carrie corrected. "But I'm close."

"Where are you?"

"Fairbanks. I just landed." Carrie had caught the first available flight out of Seattle after meeting with Joan. "So, listen, if I'm not back in Chicago on Monday, make up an excuse, will you?"

"You don't want me to tell Nash you're hot on the trail of Finn Dalton?"

"Not yet. I want to present the article as a done deal."

"I can't believe you were actually able to track him down," Sophie said excitedly.

"Don't get ahead of me; I still don't have that interview. Sorry, I need to go."

"Good luck. I've got my fingers crossed for you."

"Thanks." After ending the call, she stuck her cell phone in the outside pocket of her purse and made her way through the small airport, looking for the hangar where the bush pilots parked. All she had was Sawyer's name, and she wasn't even sure if it was his first or last. It took her awhile to locate the hangar. She asked around until she found someone willing to talk to her.

Clearly she looked enough like a city girl with her full-length double-breasted gray wool coat, fashionable boots, and earmuffs for the pilots and mechanics to recognize she was another pesky reporter in search of the elusive Finn Dalton. She was barely able to get two words out of her mouth before she got the cold shoulder.

"I'm looking for a pilot named Sawyer," she asked a man inside the hangar, doing her best to hide her frustration. He looked like a mechanic, dressed in greasy coveralls. If bush pilots weren't willing to talk to her, then perhaps he would. No one seemed to want to help.

The mechanic's eyes pierced her, slowly taking her in. "What do you want Sawyer for?" he demanded.

Carrie straightened her shoulders and stood her full five feet ten inches, meeting him almost eye to eye. "I would like to hire him."

"For what?"

"A job."

With his hands braced against his hips, the mechanic regarded her skeptically. "You're another one of them reporters, aren't you?"

Carrie decided to sidestep the question. "I have something to deliver to a friend of Sawyer's, so if you'd kindly point me in his direction, I'd be most appreciative."

"A friend of his named . . ." He left it for her to fill in the blank.

Carrie's shoulders relaxed. "Finn Dalton."

"That's what I thought." Turning his back on her, he walked completely around the outside of his plane, running his hand over the structure as though checking for something, although Carrie couldn't imagine what.

She wasn't giving up. "Can you tell me if Mr. Sawyer is in the area now, or when I can expect to find him?"

"Ah, so it's *Mr. Sawyer* now?"

Carrie ignored his tone and the question.

"I have something to give Finn Dalton."

"Do you, now? And what might that be? A headache?"

*Very funny.* She ignored that comment, although her patience was wearing thin. "It's something from his mother."

"And his mother's name is?" he asked, whirling around unexpectedly and almost colliding with her.

"Joan," she said quickly. "Joan Finnegan Dalton Reese."

The mechanic regarded her for several moments, studying her, his eyes boring into hers. "I'm Sawyer O'Halloran."

"You're Sawyer?"

"In the flesh."

After a long flight, Carrie was tired and hungry and anxious. "I want to hire you to take me to Finn Dalton."

Shaking his head, Sawyer muttered something indecipherable and walked away. "You and every other reporter who has been nosing around here."

Carrie hurried after him. "I'm serious, and I'll pay you anything reasonable if you'll take me to him. You can wait while I talk to Finn. I won't be long, I promise."

"Just as I thought. When will you people give it up? Although I have to admit you're cleverer than most, bringing up his mother."

"I'm telling you the truth. I have something to give him from her."

"Sure you do," Sawyer commented, continuing to walk away from her.

Carrie chased after him, dragging her suitcase. She had to duck her head in order to walk beneath the Cessna's wing. "It's his father's wedding band. Joan asked me to deliver it to Finn." She hated the desperate pleading quality to her voice, but she had to convince Sawyer she was legitimate.

Sawyer hesitated. "Show me the ring."

"Okay." She slid the purse strap off her shoulder and dug inside for the ring, which was wrapped in a tissue inside a plastic bag. Once it was free, she handed it to Sawyer. "His name, Paul Dalton, is engraved on the inside, along with Joan's name and the date of their wedding."

Sawyer carefully examined the gold band, and then Carrie, before returning the ring. "There's a storm due. I'm heading back to Hard Luck in fifteen minutes. I'll land on the lake outside Finn's cabin and return in the morning or whenever, depending on this storm. Is that agreeable?"

"Yes, perfect." At this point, Carrie would have agreed to practically anything.

"Finn isn't going to like this, so I'll radio him you're coming."

"I don't expect he'll have the welcome mat out."

"You've got two things against you."

"Is that all?"

"First, you're a woman, and second, you're a reporter. Make that three things."

"Three?"

"Yes. You're bringing him something from his mother. He doesn't want any reminders of her."

"So she said." Curiosity got the best of her. "Not that I want you to change your mind, but can you tell me why you're helping me?"

The bush pilot shrugged. "I'll probably regret it. Finn's a good friend, but it's time he broadened his horizons some, and you, pretty lady, might be just the ticket."

"Whatever the reason, I'm grateful."

"Finn will probably stop speaking to me, but he'll get over it eventually," Sawyer continued. "I feel I should warn you, though; he's bound to be as inviting as a wolverine."

"Got it. Any other advice?"

Sawyer scratched the side of his head. "I wouldn't start off mentioning the ring and his mother." He gave her the once-over a second time. "You pack anything practical for the weather?"

"I live in Chicago. It freezes there."

He snorted as if to cover a laugh. "You've got fifteen minutes. Make use of them." He pointed in the direction of the airport, and Carrie took off running. She wasn't sure what she'd need, but with the help of the clerk picked up a couple of pieces of gear, including a hat and thick scarf. It seemed extravagant to purchase anything else, seeing that she intended to be in Alaska only a short while.

By the time she returned, Sawyer had moved the plane out of the hangar and had the engine running. "You ready?" he asked.

Because she was winded and excited, she only nodded.

"Okay, climb inside. We need to get going."

"Right now?" She'd hoped to have a few moments to gather herself.

"Yes, now," he snapped. "There's limited light, and with the coming storm, that window is closing. Ready or not, I'm leaving."

"I'm ready." Carrie had never flown in a private plane, but that one small detail wasn't about to stop her. She eyed the Cessna, sucked in a deep breath, and loaded her suitcase. It wasn't easy climbing inside and locking the passenger door. Carrie was relieved she'd worn her jeans, and thankfully her boots had only a moderate heel.

Within a few minutes they were airborne, circling the airport and heading due north. Carrie clung to her purse as if that would save her from imminent danger and held her breath several times when the plane rocked after encountering moderate turbulence. Sawyer had handed her a pair of headphones, but he wasn't much for conversation, preoccupied as he was with flying the plane. He radioed Finn twice but wasn't able to reach him. Although Sawyer didn't say so, Carrie had the feeling he already regretted agreeing to this. Fearing anything she said might do more harm than good, she remained silent until it was clear that he was preparing to land.

"Where's the airstrip?" she asked, studying the landscape below. In the dim light, all she could see were snow and trees.

"Airstrip?" Sawyer repeated incredulously. "I'm not landing on any strip. Didn't I already mention I'd be landing on a lake?"

Set on convincing him to fly her to Finn, Carrie didn't remember that part of their conversation. A lake? A frozen lake? Peering through the window, she couldn't make out anything but snow. She gasped out loud when the plane's wheels bounced against the ice and skidded sideways out of control.

Sawyer didn't cut the engine but guided the Cessna to the lake's center and turned toward her.

"Under normal conditions, I'd escort you to Finn's cabin. Unfortunately, I'm headed directly into that storm, and I don't have the time to spare. You can see his cabin over there," he said, pointing in the distance.

Carrie squinted in the fading light. "Is it far?"

"You'll happen upon it soon enough. If Finn isn't there, make yourself at home, and have him contact me." He snickered. "Actually, no need, he'll be in touch, I'm sure. You going to be okay?"

Carrie nodded, swallowed hard, and put on a good front. "I was a Girl Scout. I'll be fine." She could see the outline of the cabin through the thick, fat flakes that had already started to fall. Sawyer needed to get back in the air as quickly as possible.

"Good luck," he said, and it sounded as if he meant it.

"We'll square up with what I owe you when you return tomorrow."

"Sure, whatever. But like I said, with the weather, it might be a day or two."

Carrie bit into the soft flesh of her inner lip. "Okay." She was grateful he had brought her this far and would count her blessings.

He hit the throttle, which was her signal to get going. Carrie opened the plane's door and climbed out, but not with a lot of grace. She retrieved her small suitcase and the bag of gear she'd bought and stood back as the plane immediately accelerated across the frozen lake. The wind and snow whipped across Carrie's face with such ferocity that it felt as if she were being stuck with needles.

Other than her brief time in the hangar when she'd first met Sawyer, she hadn't been exposed to the Alaskan elements, and they were as brutal as the bush pilot had warned. Her coat, which had been all the protection she needed in Chicago, felt useless. Already she was so cold she had started to shake. Within moments her toes had lost all feeling. Wrapping her new scarf around her head and face, she started walking in the direction of the cabin.

With the plane airborne now, the thin layer of snow settled down on the thick ice, and in the distance Carrie saw a twisting tail of smoke. That had to be coming from Finn's cabin.

Carrie hunched her shoulders as close to her head as she could manage, and even through the protection of her gloves, it felt as if her hands were exposed to the raw elements. The ice was uneven, and dragging her suitcase wasn't an easy task. With her hands numb, she twice dropped the suitcase handle and had to stop and pick it back up.

She hadn't even met Finn and already she'd started to feel as if this was a terrible mistake. Everything had happened so quickly, and when she did meet him she wasn't sure what she would say to convince him to give her an interview.

Suddenly it started to snow with such ferocity that she couldn't see more than a few feet in front of her. The wind drove it sideways, and with her head bowed she struggled against the elements until she heard what sounded like a wild beast. Looking up, Carrie squinted, and what she saw caused her heart to shoot up to her throat. It was an animal, a wolf, and he was racing toward her at an alarming pace.

Dropping her suitcase, Carrie did the only thing she could think to do. She started running. The wind made it nearly impossible to make headway as she strained against the force of it.

Then it happened. She stumbled and fell face-first onto the ice.

Before she could right herself, the wolf was nearly on top of her.

Screaming, she twisted around and bunched her fists, determined to do what she could to save her life.

# Chapter 3

"Hennessey, sit."

Carrie felt the animal's warm breath against her neck and then didn't. Struggling to sit upright, she turned to see a man walking toward her across the ice. The wind swirled the snow around him, obliterating his features, but his strides were long and powerful. The animal she'd assumed was a wolf appeared now to be a large dog. Hennessey sat on his haunches, awaiting his master.

His master.

This could only be Finn Dalton.

When he reached her, the hulk of a man loomed over her like a beast in his own right. His face was nearly obscured by protective weather gear and a full beard, but his eyes, deep and dark, cut through her the way a diamond slices through rock. As Carrie gazed up at him, in those first few breathless moments, he seemed more intimidating than the wolf/dog had been.

"Who are you?" he shouted, but his voice was carried away by the wind. Leaning down, he reached for her arm, pulling her to her feet. Upright now, her boots slipped against the freshly fallen snow, and she would have toppled a second time if he hadn't held her in place. Shaking his head in what could be described only as disgust, he grabbed her about the waist and tucked her under his arm as if she were no bigger than a rag doll. Before she could protest, he started walking toward the cabin, eating up the distance with angry strides. Carrie was perpendicular to the ground, so all she could see was the snow on the lake. By now, the hair that had escaped her hat was frozen tendrils that slapped against the tender skin of her cheeks. Hennessey obediently followed. Carrie thought to protest and demand that he put her down, but she knew it would do no good. He probably wouldn't be able to hear her.

"M-y, m-y suitcase," she shouted, or tried. Then she noticed that he had that and her shopping bag in his other hand. His strength astonished her. He carried her with one arm as if she weighed next to nothing.

Hennessey trailed behind them, keeping a careful watch on her. Carrie had the impression that if Finn were to mutter one word, Hennessey would happily make a meal out of her.

By the time they reached the cabin, Carrie was shaking from head to foot. Finn kicked the door closed and set her down, but she found it impossible to stand upright. Gripping her by the waist, he promptly placed her in a chair in the kitchen area.

Then he faced her with his feet apart and his hands braced against his hips. "Who the hell are you, and what are you doing here?"

Carrie did her best to answer, but her teeth chattered so hard that speaking coherently was a lost cause. In the cozy warmth of the cabin her frozen hair started to thaw, dripping cold water against her shoulders as tight ringlets formed about her head. Thankfully, the huge wood-burning stove warmed the cabin. The log cabin was a marvel, and she did her best to take in as much of it as she could. From the outside Finn's rustic home didn't look like much, and she was pleasantly surprised by the interior, with plenty of bookshelves, braided rugs, and large furniture.

"What are you doing here?" he demanded a second time.

"A . . . well, my name is . . ."

"I don't care what your name is."

As though he couldn't bear to look at her a moment longer, he filled a pot with water and then placed it atop the old-fashioned cast-iron cookstove. She continued to shiver, bracing her glove-covered hands across her body. In some ways, Carrie felt as if she were actually holding herself together.

Finn studied her as if he'd never seen anyone more pathetic in his life. "Get out of those wet clothes," he told her gruffly.

He didn't need to remind her that her outfit wasn't suited to the frigid weather. Everything had happened so quickly. Just the day before, she'd met his mother, and then there were the last-minute flight arrangements to Fairbanks. She'd arrived mid-morning, and then there was the roller-coaster ride in the bush plane. Although it was still afternoon, the sun had already gone down.

Still shaking with cold and shock, Carrie removed her wool coat and unwound the newly purchased scarf from her neck. Next she attempted to unzip her boots, but her frozen fingers refused to cooperate. Finn walked over to where she sat, got down on one knee, and undid them for her. Pulling off her boots, he set them by the stove to thaw and then disappeared behind a fabric door, only to return a couple of moments later with a pair of thick wool socks. Still shivering, Carrie managed to pull them on.

Without asking permission, Finn opened her suitcase and sifted through its contents, shook his head, and slammed it shut. She had a couple of thick sweaters, but little else suitable for the harsh Alaskan elements. Once again he disappeared into the other room and returned with a wool shirt, which she slipped on even though it was far too large for her.

Not a word was exchanged between them. She watched him move, wanting to remember everything she could about him for her article. Right away she noticed that while he was a large man, he moved with a grace and ease that defied his size. His hair was as dark as her own, and shoulder length. Unfortunately, his full beard hid his face. Even without seeing him clean shaven, she doubted that he would be considered traditionally handsome. His nose was a bit too large and his mouth a tad too thin. While he didn't appear to be hunk-calendar material, she found the raw vitality surrounding him strongly appealing.

Although they hadn't spoken, she sensed his irritation and his curiosity. He had probably already guessed she was a reporter, which was why he hadn't pursued his questions. One look told her he was determined not to give her any information she could publish.

When the water was thoroughly heated, Finn brewed coffee and without a word set a mug on the table in front of her. Carrie took it and held on to it with both hands. The first sip scalded her lips, but it was so deliciously hot that she barely minded. Finn remained on the far side of the room, close to the hot stove, as if to keep as much distance between them as possible.

Taking careful note of what she saw, Carrie realized that most everything inside the cabin had been made by hand. The space was compact but utilized beautifully. The kitchen area, complete with sink and countertop, a few open-faced cupboards, the cast-iron stove, and a table with four chairs, flowed naturally into a cozy sitting area. Hennessey lay on an oval-shaped braided rug close to the warmth of the stove. Two rocking chairs rested on either side, with dry wood stacked close by, and a sofa rested against another wall. The windows, of which there were two—one in the kitchen and another in the living area—had coverings that were pulled tightly closed. The cabin had lights, which she assumed were powered by a generator. What she found encouraging were the book-cases built against the walls, which were jam-packed. From what she could see, Finn Dalton was a reader.

When possible, she'd check out the titles, which were sure to give her insight into this man.

"My name is Carrie," she offered, hoping that by being open and friendly he'd be willing to chat. "Carrie Slayton."

Finn ignored her and sat down with his back facing her.

Fully capable of moving now, Carrie stood and, taking the coffee with her, claimed the second chair. The heat from the stove felt glorious. "I apologize for arriving unannounced."

"Who brought you?" The question was clipped, angry.

"Sawyer. He tried to reach you, but you didn't pick up and—"

"How much did you pay him?" he asked, cutting her off.

"Well, nothing yet. I told him I'd square up with him in the morning when he returns to pick me up."

Finn snickered.

Carrie wasn't sure what that meant. "We discussed terms, and I found his price reasonable."

"What did he charge? Thirty pieces of silver?"

"No, no, it was nothing like that."

For the first time she noticed a small nook on the

other side of the room. He had another table set up there, with a lone chair. On the table was a computer and what she assumed was a radio. If she'd had his email address, she might have been able to convince him to give her the interview. Then again, probably not.

"Your cabin is amazing . . . all the conveniences. You actually have a computer, but then I shouldn't be surprised, right? I know that you worked with your publisher via email."

Nothing. This one-sided conversation wasn't going the least bit well.

"I read your book," she said, trying again. "It was wonderful. The stories are detailed and rich. You make the reader feel part of the story as well. That's a rare gift. My dad read your book, too, long before me. In fact, Mom mentioned that he purchased two additional copies as gifts this Christmas. *Alone* is still on the best-seller lists and has been for months, but then you probably already know that." She realized she was chattering away and stopped.

"I'm grateful you found me when you did," she said, trying again after several tense moments of silence. "Sawyer wanted to stay, but the storm was fast approaching and he needed to get back to Bad Luck." What an unusual name for a town.

"Hard Luck," he corrected.

"Right. Hard Luck." That wasn't much better. It was difficult to maintain this cheerful facade with little to no feedback.

"I bet you'd like to know how I found you." She thought it might work out better if she asked questions.

Nothing. Unfortunately, she'd supposed wrong. Finn Dalton had no interest in speaking to her, no matter how she directed the conversation.

"If you don't want to talk, that's fine, I understand," she said with a labored sigh. "I mean, I've intruded on your life and it's unbelievably rude of me, I know."

They sat in silence for several minutes, but the tension between them was so strong it felt like overactive bass pounding from a speaker. Carrie was quickly losing patience. She hadn't come this far and jumped through all these hoops to be thwarted now.

"You wouldn't believe all the different ways I tried to find you," she said. It felt like a shallow victory now, seeing how uncooperative Finn was. But then, this should have been expected. While she was jubilant, he, on the other hand, was hostile.

Hennessey kept his gaze focused directly on her. "Good boy," she said, and made sure her voice was soft and cajoling. "You're a friendly dog, aren't you?"

Like his master, Hennessey gave no indication that he'd heard. The canine's eyes steadily regarded her, watching her every move. With Finn freezing her out, she looked to his companion for some connection. At this point she was willing to accept whatever Hennessey was willing to give her.

"I hope you know you practically gave me a heart attack, racing up on me like that," she told the dog. She bent forward and stretched out her hand, making sure he understood that all she wanted was to pet him.

"He bites," Finn warned, and from the way he clipped out the words, it seemed he would welcome the sight.

Hennessey's gaze flickered to Finn and then back to Carrie.

"Are you a big, bad wolf?" Carrie asked Hennessey softly.

The dog's eyes met hers, and then Hennessey moved to rest his chin on his paws. Then, to her utter amazement, he wagged his tail. Just one wag, one single shift to indicate that he no longer considered her a threat. It was enough to make Carrie want to shout with delight.

"I'm friendly, Hennessey, really friendly. Can we be friends?" Once again she extended her hand for the dog to see.

Again, Finn warned her. "I wouldn't do that if I were you."

Carrie slowly withdrew her hand.

Hennessey lifted his head and looked up at her and then his tail started to move, this time to a full wag, as if to tell her he was willing to trust Carrie if she was willing to trust him.

"Another traitor," Finn muttered under his breath.

"Sawyer isn't a traitor," Carrie insisted. "And Hennessey isn't, either."

Finn snorted and then sipped his coffee.

"Finn . . . Mr. Dalton," she said, trying again. She didn't mean to sound so familiar, and at the same time, "Mr. Dalton" came off as much too formal. "As you've guessed, I'm a reporter. I write for the *Chicago Herald*. Actually, I cover the society page. It's not my favorite subject, but I was grateful to get the job. I'm a good reporter, and I wanted an opportunity to prove that I was capable of writing something other than who was seen where and with whom. I am sick to death of writing about meaningless parties and who's getting married and who's breaking up. So sick that I was ready to quit, and then my editor, who's been in the business thirty years, said I could have any assignment I wanted if I could manage to interview you. Little did I know how difficult finding you would be."

Once she'd started explaining, she couldn't seem to stop. Her hope was that once Finn heard her story he'd be willing to cooperate.

Eventually he'd have to give an interview to someone, and it might as well be her. She was the one who'd found a way to reach him; that should prove something. He had to know his book was practically a phenomenon and the public was curious to know more about him.

"If I was able to find you, then others will, too . . . eventually."

He glared at her as if to refute her words.

"Your book is amazing, and your readers want to meet the man behind *Alone*. And really, who could blame them? Surely you realized when you submitted the book what it would mean?"

He remained unmoved, so Carrie tried another tactic. Perhaps he would feel sorry for her. "I gave up spending Thanksgiving with my family in order to find you, but it'd be worth every one of my vacation days and a lot more if you were willing to give me an interview." Studying him, she could tell he wasn't the least bit concerned.

"Are you looking for sympathy from me?"

"No, of course not . . . well, maybe, just a little."

He briefly closed his eyes and shook his head.

"I'll tell you what," she said in the same cheerful tone she'd used earlier. "I'll let you preview the piece, give it your stamp of approval. If you don't like it, then it won't get printed."

"Do you honestly expect me to believe that?"

"Well, yes, of course. I'm a woman of my word."

"I've yet to meet one who is." His words dripped with disdain. Snickering softly, he walked over to where the computer and the radio were set up. Pulling out the chair, he sat down, flipped a couple of switches, and put on headphones. It didn't take Carrie long to figure out his call was to Sawyer.

Although Carrie could hear only one side of the conversation, it was enough. She was the main topic of interest.

"If this is a joke, I'm not laughing. Over."

From Finn's reaction, Sawyer was apparently amused.

"You're way off base," Finn shouted into the microphone. "Having a woman here, let alone a woman reporter, isn't my idea of doing me a favor. I don't care who she is or who she knows. Over."

Sawyer replied, but Carrie couldn't make out what he said.

"I don't want her here, and that's putting it mildly. Over."

Silence followed. Finn rubbed his hand over his beard in what she could only assume was frustration.

"You have twenty-four hours to come get her. Over."

He slapped his hand against the top of the table. "No . . . I don't care about any damn storm. You brought this on yourself. Over."

Carrie was worried. She really didn't want to remain with Finn in this isolated cabin any longer than it took to get what she needed for the article. The sooner Sawyer came for her, the better. She needed to be back to work in Chicago. With the holidays coming up, there were any number of social events she'd been assigned to cover. If worse came to worst and she was stuck in Alaska, Nash would forgive her once she handed him the interview with Finn. Even in the short amount of time she'd been with him, she could relay a number of interesting details about the man.

"Twenty-four hours is my limit. Over." Finn ended the conversation with what sounded very much like a threat.

Carrie was left to wonder what he would do if Sawyer didn't return for her in the prescribed amount of time.

Surely Finn wouldn't put her out in the cold to deal with the elements alone. Would he?

When he finished he removed the headphones and turned off the radio.

Carrie remained frozen, hardly knowing what to do or say, so she did nothing.

Finn reached for his mug and drank down the last dregs of his coffee, and then delivered the empty cup to the kitchen sink. Carrie got out of the chair. Her own coffee was finished, so she followed him, the movement of the wool socks against the cabin floor nearly silent. Unfortunately she was closer behind him than either of them realized, because when he turned, he nearly mowed her down.

With his hands braced against her upper arms, he glared down at her, a deep frown etched into his forehead. "Stay out of my way." Each word was distinctly spoken, leaving her in no doubt as to the strength of his feelings.

"Sorry . . . that was an accident." She stuttered slightly, and while she attempted to figure how best to get his cooperation, Finn grabbed his coat, hat, and gloves, and after getting everything on, promptly walked outside.

Carrie stared at the closed door, too stunned to move. She'd had such high hopes for this interview, but if this "coffee time" was any indication of what was to follow, then she was going down in flames.

Hennessey remained by the stove, seemingly content to stay by the warm fire. Carrie got down on the rug next to him, sitting with her legs folded and her chin braced against her knees.

"He doesn't like me," she told the dog.

Hennessey lifted his head to gaze at her.

"I can't say that I blame him. I barged into his life, and now I'm paying the price."

To her delight, Hennessey lifted his chin and then rested it on top of her foot. Although Finn had warned her that he might bite, she gently placed her hand on the top of his head. After giving him a moment to adjust to the feel of her touch, she stroked the length of his spine.

"You're nothing like the big, bad wolf Finn makes you out to be," she whispered. "You're a big puffball."

Well, at least Finn's dog liked her, and for now that was enough. She continued stroking his fur, burrowing her fingers into his thick coat. "Maybe I should interview you instead," she suggested quietly. "How does that sound?"

The large wolf/dog didn't indicate his feelings on the matter one way or another.

"Hennessey, tell me, what's it like . . ."

The door opened again, and Finn came in along with a blast of frigid air and an armload of wood. Thankfully, he shut the door and latched it. He set the wood down by the stove, stacking it for the night.

"Can I do anything to help?" Carrie asked.

"Leave."

"I can't," she whispered.

"Don't I know it."

"I'd hoped . . . I'd assumed that Sawyer would fly me in to meet you, and the two of us could briefly chat and then I'd be on my way, mission accomplished."

"And now I'm stuck with you."

"Yes, I know, and I apologize." Seeing that he didn't welcome her help with the evening meal, she felt the least she could do was get her carry-on bag out of the way.

"Is there someplace you'd like me to put my suitcase?" she asked.

"You mean like in a guest bedroom?" he asked with more than a hint of sarcasm.

"Well, yes."

He snickered. "There's only one bedroom, and only one bed, and I'm telling you right now I'm not sleeping on the sofa."

# Chapter 4

This was an unwelcome predicament, and Finn wasn't the least bit happy. The biggest shock was that Sawyer had turned on him. Sawyer O'Halloran was a friend, a good friend, and beyond reproach . . . until now. Their brief conversation left more questions than it provided answers. The woman had something for him, Sawyer claimed, but to this point she'd kept it to herself. Finn hadn't questioned his friend, although the temptation had been strong. Whatever it was had convinced Sawyer to fly her in. To his credit, Sawyer had attempted to reach him.

After several hours of tense silence, Finn loaded wood into the stove and brought out the leftover moose-meat stew for his dinner. He glanced at Carrie and grumbled under his breath. She was a pretty thing, with hair dark enough to be called chocolate and startling blue eyes, although he tried not to notice anything about her. Women like Carrie Slayton were sure to leave a string of broken hearts in their wake, and Finn was determined not to be one of them. He noticed that she kept touching her head. It appeared to have something to do with her hair, which had twisted into springy ringlets after it'd gotten wet in the snow. She seemed to be self-conscious about it, waiting for him to tease her. He wouldn't. Truth be known, he found her hair to be one of the most attractive features about her.

Not good. Noticing anything about the woman in his cabin was a sign of weakness, and Finn refused to allow her to take up one iota of consideration.

As much as he hated to admit it, what she said about granting her the interview made sense. If she'd been able to find him, then other reporters would as well, sooner or later. He'd ignored that inevitability longer than he should have. Not that her argument had persuaded him—nothing would. Finn wrote the book to share his love of the wilderness and to fill the long, lonely hours of the winter solitude. Never in his wildest dreams had he expected it to be such an overwhelming success.

Thankfully, he'd done all the legal transactions through an attorney, with the stipulation that he maintain his privacy. He hadn't agreed to a single interview, regardless of repeated attempts by his publisher. Despite how it looked, Finn wasn't a recluse but simply a man who enjoyed his solitude. He wasn't about to disrupt his life and become a media darling.

Finn didn't dislike women; he simply didn't trust a single one of them. Those were lessons he'd learned the hard way. His father was never the same after his mother left. He'd grown bitter and hard, and drummed those lessons into Finn. Later Finn had discovered on his own what his father had tried to tell him. Women were fickle and not worth the trouble they caused in a man's life. He'd fallen for Pamela, but she'd hurt him the same way his mother had hurt his father. Thankfully, Finn had learned early in their relationship that Pamela wasn't trustworthy. It embarrassed him to remember the way she'd played him. Finn made the mistake of believing he was falling in love with her only to learn she was married and bored and looking for a little action on the side while her husband was overseas. Finn was willing to admit he enjoyed being with women, but he knew better than to involve his heart.

He did feel bad about the sleeping situation. But

Carrie was the one who'd come uninvited and unannounced. What she'd done was stupid and dangerous, and there were consequences. Finn refused to give her his bed, although the idea of sharing it with her was fairly tempting. He quickly shook his head, casting the image out of his mind.

Despite his best efforts, his gaze wandered back to her and her beautiful hair. Who was he kidding? It wasn't only her hair that attracted him; she was a knockout. Little wonder Sawyer hadn't been able to refuse her. No doubt she had a string of boyfriends as long as the Alaska shoreline.

Frowning, he realized he wasn't the only one who noticed how attractive she was. Hennessey had cozied right up to her. Finn wouldn't have believed it if he hadn't seen it with his own eyes. Generally, Hennessey didn't take kindly to strangers. It seemed his faithful mutt wasn't immune to her charms, either.

As far as he was concerned, the sooner Carrie Slayton was out of his hair, the better.

Carrie swallowed hard as she surveyed the cozy living room off the kitchen. The couch was old and lumpy, but the only alternative was the floor. "Where would you like me to sleep?" She sat down on the couch, testing it, her hands at her sides. It would do in a pinch, she supposed, and it would be more comfortable than the hard floor.

"Wherever you want. The choice is yours, although I should warn you Hennessey considers the sofa his."

Finn remained in the kitchen, and from what she could see he appeared to be putting dinner together, heating a pot on the stove. Although it was early evening, it seemed much later. The aroma from the stew was heavenly. Carrie's stomach growled, reminding her that it'd been several hours since she'd last eaten, and that had been pretzels the airline handed out during the flight. In her rush to get to the airport, she'd skipped breakfast.

"Getting stuck here for the night wasn't what I planned, either," she reminded him. "I don't appreciate being here any more than you want me," she said, and then felt she should explain further. "I need to be back in Chicago. Sophie will cover for me, but . . ." She stopped when it was clear he had no interest in listening to her concerns.

He paused, glanced up, and said, "You should have considered that earlier."

The wind continued to howl and hiss, reminding her that it could be days before Sawyer would be able to return. This was quickly turning into an unmitigated disaster.

She was deep in her worries, and dinner proved to be a miserable affair. Finn served the stew, which he, thankfully, shared with her. The meat didn't have a familiar taste, and Carrie decided she was better off not knowing what it was. Bear? Walrus? Mountain goat? For his part, Finn seemed to think if he pretended she was invisible he could completely ignore her. He made it clear he wasn't interested in conversation. Carrie took the hint and ate her meal in silence. When she'd finished, she politely complimented his efforts and thanked him.

Almost immediately after dinner, Finn went into the bedroom and returned a few minutes later with two thick blankets and a pillow. Without a word, he handed them to her.

"Thank you," she said, taking them from him and holding them against her chest. He might have the personality of a rattlesnake, but she wasn't about to let his bad mood affect her.

Apologizing to Hennessey, she made her bed on the sofa, scooting it as close to the stove as she dared. As soon as she lay down, Hennessey leaped up and snuggled next to her legs. Stretching out her arm, she welcomed the canine's warmth. This was probably the earliest she'd gone to bed since she was a toddler.

Although she should be exhausted, Carrie found her mind racing. "He's not going to give me the interview," she told the dog, rolling onto her back and staring up at the log beams of the ceiling.

"Maybe I will interview you," she said, and gently petted Hennessey's head.

The dog rested his chin against her knee in a move that both comforted and warmed her.

"Okay, Hennessey, tell me what it's like living with the great Finn Dalton, esteemed author of *Alone*."

She waited, pretending to listen to his answer.

"You can't mean to say you actually like spending countless hours with such a cantankerous owner? I'm wrong, you say, and he really isn't as bad as I assume? Frankly, I find that hard to believe! Oh, I'm sure you're right, Finn Dalton can be civil, but unfortunately he sees me as an evil threat and he wants to boot me out of here as fast as he can. I know, I know, it's a shame we couldn't have reached an understanding. It's only a matter of time, you know, before others track him down."

Again she paused as though taking in the dog's comments.

"Yes, I hear you. To you he's a good guy, but to me

he's rude and arrogant and a narcissist. Oh, sorry, *narcissist* is a big word. It means he's completely hung up on himself."

A loud snort came from the other room, which was a sure sign Finn was listening in on their conversation.

"Okay, I realize you have a few questions for me, too. Ask away."

She pretended to be listening before she answered. "Like I explained earlier, America is interested in learning what they can about the man who wrote *Alone*. They see Finn as some sort of hero. Little do they know what he's really like."

She paused and waited for a couple of moments. "Oh, you want to know how I was able to find him when so many others have failed? Sawyer asked me the same question. He told me a handful of reporters have tried to bribe him and a couple of other bush pilots to help locate Finn, but none of Finn's friends would betray him." She yawned as if she were ready to call it a night.

"Answer the dog's question." Finn stood in the doorway, holding back the fabric partition. "I'm curious to know what you have for me that convinced Sawyer to bring you here. He's a good friend, and I know he wouldn't be easily swayed."

Carrie sat upright and wrapped her arms around her

bent knees. So this is what it took to get the mighty Finn to open up. "If you must know, it was what I told him about your mother."

"My mother," Finn repeated slowly. "What does she have to do with any of this?"

"I found her, and—"

"You searched out my mother?" he demanded in what came across as anger mingled with restraint.

"Well, yes. So have others, but I was able to convince her to talk to me. Your mother and I had a good chat, and—"

Finn took two steps into the room and braced his hands against his hips, looking at her as if she were the lowest of the low. "You actually talked to my mother?"

"I just said as much, and she—"

"I don't care what she said. I want nothing to do with her."

Carrie sighed, feeling wretched for Joan when all she wanted was to connect with her son. "She told me that you'd probably react like this the minute I mentioned her to you."

"She walked out on my father and me—"

"Oh, come on, Finn, you have to know it's more complicated than that. She loves you, and your father didn't give her many options."

"Listen, Ms. Busybody, this is none of your business, so stay out of it." He marched back to the bedroom and pushed aside the curtain with such force she was surprised it didn't rip in half.

Carrie was ready to wash her hands of this obstinate, unfeeling man. He was unreasonable, unforgiving . . . and a dozen more unflattering words that circled her mind. Lying back down, she stared up at the ceiling. Hennessey remained at her side.

"He really has mother issues, doesn't he?" she told the dog, lowering her voice to a whisper.

"I heard that."

Carrie ignored him, seeing how well he'd managed to pretend she didn't exist. "His heart must be as cold as ice not to care about his own mother."

"Stay out of it, Carrie."

She ignored that, too.

"His attitude toward her explains a great deal. It seems to me Finnegan Dalton has distinct abandonment issues, right along with issues regarding all women."

He laughed as though he found her analysis amusing.

"Why else would he choose to live in the Alaska wilderness alone?"

"You think you're clever, don't you?" he muttered.

"But all that is probably just the tip of the iceberg."

"Would you stop!"

"*Alone* is right." She raised her voice to be sure he heard her loud and clear. "He's probably been running away his entire life. Then he had to go and make the mistake of writing a bestselling book that captured the public's attention. How unfortunate for him."

Silence.

The blizzard howled outside the door, and Carrie was grateful Hennessey had chosen to stay with her. She punched the pillow several times and then lay back down, pulling the thick blanket over her shoulders and forcing her eyes closed. Finn Dalton could thank his lucky stars she wasn't writing the article on him right that minute. She couldn't think of a single flattering comment she could make about this ill-mannered man.

The minutes ticked past, but as hard as she tried, Carrie couldn't fall sleep. The sofa was uncomfortable, and Finn had made her so angry the adrenaline pumped through her, making it impossible to relax.

"He hates all women, doesn't he?" she asked Hennessey, keeping her voice low and soft.

The dog lifted his head, and she almost expected an answer.

"Not true," Finn insisted. He stood in the doorway to the bedroom again, filling it with his bulk.

Ah, so he hadn't been able to fall asleep, either. "Is so," she returned with equal fervor. "How else do you explain yourself? Your mother was given very few options. My goodness, Finn, think about it. She was a southern belle; these harsh elements were too much for her. She wanted to compromise, but your father wouldn't hear of it. She told me it broke her heart to leave you behind, but you and your father were so close she couldn't bear to separate you. When you chose to stay with your father, she could have insisted, could have taken the matter to the courts, but she didn't. She bowed to your wishes even though it broke her heart."

"She told you all this, did she?"

"Yes, and that's not all. She mentioned how rude you were to her when your father died. She attended his funeral to make what amends she could, and you rejected her." Carrie's jaw tightened just thinking about the unkind way Finn had behaved toward his mother.

"She had no right to be there. She remarried."

"She loved your father, and she loves you." It was beyond Carrie's imagination that Finn would continue to shut his mother out, especially after losing his father. "You were a boy when she left. You only heard one side of the story."

"So did you, and frankly, what's between my mother and me is none of your concern."

He was right; Carrie was butting her head into areas that had nothing to do with writing the article. However, now that she'd started, she couldn't seem to stop. "Your mother wants you in her life. You're her only child."

"She should have thought of that twenty-five years ago." As though he was exhausted from their argument, he slowly shook his head and whispered, "Just go to sleep, would you?"

She was about to mention how uncomfortable the sofa was, but he might assume she was looking for an invitation to join him in his bed. Nothing could be further from the truth. "I'm trying, but you make me so angry that I can't think straight."

"Try harder." The curtain between the two rooms swayed as he whirled around and returned to bed.

Carrie didn't know how long it was before she managed to sleep. At some point in the night she woke from the cold and drew the thick blankets more snugly about her shoulders. Later, she was overly warm and kicked them free from her jean-clad legs.

At about midnight, she opened her eyes to find Finn standing by the stove, feeding it the wood he'd brought in earlier.

The next thing she knew, he was gently waking her. "You can have the bed now."

She blinked up at him without understanding. He was fully dressed, and while it surely must be close to morning, the only light that showed came from the fire in the stove.

Finn led her into the bedroom, and once she'd crawled into the ultracomfortable feather bed, he covered her with thick blankets. "I'll be gone for a while."

"Okay," she mumbled, already half asleep. Surrounded by warmth and comfort, she thought sleeping on this soft mattress was heavenly.

When she woke, it was still dark. She quickly put on every bit of clothing that she could fit into until her arms were so thick with two long-sleeved shirts and two sweaters that she could barely bend her elbows.

Although she'd never cooked on a cast-iron stove, it didn't seem that difficult. The coffeepot sat on the stove top, but she was unable to get water from the faucet. Once she got the fire going, she opened the cabin door. She blinked at the cold that seemed to come at her like a giant fist. It stole her breath, but she managed to pack the coffeepot with snow and then quickly came back inside. Searching through Finn's cupboards, she found coffee and quickly assembled a pot. The coffee had just finished brewing when she heard Hennessey bark.

Finn was back.

Carrie couldn't imagine where he'd gone or what he'd been doing, especially in the snow. She automatically reached for a second mug and filled it. Finn came in the door, followed by Hennessey, who instantly went to her side. She bent down and petted her newfound friend. Finn seemed surprised to see her up and about.

"The storm has let up," he murmured. "But not enough for Sawyer to fly."

"Oh." Carrie had been afraid that was the case. She handed him a mug of steaming brew.

"You made coffee," he said, as if this was some gargantuan feat.

"Yes." It was one thing to get into a sparring match with him in the dead of night and quite another to do so when they were standing face-to-face. She'd made several accusations that she wished now had remained unsaid. It embarrassed her that she had delved into his personal life when what he did or didn't do was none of her affair.

Finn, too, seemed uneasy.

"Have you had breakfast?" she asked, although she didn't have a clue what she would cook if he hadn't. It wasn't like she had access to fresh eggs. From what little she'd picked up about life in the frozen north, being this close to the tree line meant that groceries, supplies, or anything else Finn needed would have to be flown in.

"I ate earlier. You?"

"Not yet." This strained politeness was a complete turnaround from the way they'd behaved toward each other previously. Carrie felt responsible for clearing the air, although she wasn't sure what to say or if she should even try. Perhaps it would be best to just pretend their verbal skirmish hadn't happened.

"There's some caribou jerky if you're interested. Made it myself this summer."

His attitude toward her appeared to be a bit more amicable, she noticed. "Thanks, but I'm not much of a breakfast person."

"Suit yourself."

He removed his coat and then sat down at the table with his coffee, his gaze focused on the cup as if he were reading tea leaves.

Carrie sat down across from him and decided to make an effort at conversation. "About last night . . ."

His head shot up, and his gaze narrowed significantly. "What about it?"

"I want to apologize for the things I said about you and your mother."

He bobbed his head as though to assure her all was forgiven. "I don't want to talk about it."

"Okay. But I still think you have issues with women."

"Drop it, would you?" he said between clenched teeth.

Carrie held up her hand. "You're right, sorry."

He relaxed and sipped his coffee.

"I need to do something, and I don't want to make you mad, so I'm telling you in advance."

"Now what?" he asked, as if he'd already grown tired of the conversation.

Carrie slipped the tips of her fingers into her jeans pocket. "Your mother asked me to give you this. I feel honor bound to follow through with my promise to her."

"Give me what?"

"Your father's wedding band."

His face tightened. "Keep it."

"I can't do that; a promise is a promise."

He stared across the short space between them and then smiled. "That's how you convinced Sawyer to fly you in, isn't it? You told him you had something for me, but he didn't say what and I didn't ask."

Carrie didn't feel she could or should lie. "I'm grateful Sawyer was willing to help me, but he didn't do it for me. He did it because he felt he was doing what was best for you. He's a friend, and from what I can see, a good one."

Finn snorted and rubbed his hand down his beard. "I knew it had to be something like that."

She placed the gold band in the center of the table.

"Satisfied now?" he asked.

"Yes."

His chair made a grating noise as he stood and reached for the gold band, which he carried to the front door. He opened it, letting snow and wind into the cabin before he tossed the ring with all his might into the storm.

# Chapter 5

Carrie bolted to her feet and raced through the open door, and practically dove face-first into the whirling snow. The wind blinded her but she caught a glimpse of metal and nearly fell on it in her eagerness to retrieve Paul Dalton's wedding band. Clenching the gold band tightly in the palm of her hand, Carrie battled the storm in an effort to hurry back into the house. It took all her strength to close the door against the elements. By the time she was finished she was half frozen and breathless.

"How could you be so uncaring?" Carrie demanded, glaring at Finn. Her lungs hurt from the brief time she'd been in the icy cold. Chicago was known for its brutal winters, but this frigid air was beyond anything she'd ever experienced.

"Why should I care about a wedding ring when the marriage meant nothing to my mother?" he retorted.

Carrie leaned against the door, needing its support to remain upright. Her entire body was rigid with cold and anger. She waited for a moment, letting the warmth of the room revive her enough to think clearly.

"The ring belonged to your father," she reminded him. One would think Finn would hold on to the band as a keepsake, if for no other reason than the fact that his father had once worn and treasured it.

"Dad returned it to my mother at the time of the divorce. If he didn't want it, what makes you think I would?"

"And your mother kept it, which should tell you something." Carrie didn't know why she felt such a strong need to defend his mother. In some way, it felt as though she was sticking up for herself as well as all the other women of the world.

"As far as I can determine, women are out for what they can get from a man. You don't care who you step on or who you hurt. I made the mistake of thinking I was in love once, but I won't make it again."

"All women?" Carrie challenged. He wasn't making

sense. "You see us as selfish and untrustworthy because your mother left you? And you have the nerve to tell me you don't have abandonment issues?" She resisted the urge to laugh. This guy was a real piece of work. "Have you considered counseling?"

"You think this is just about my mother. You don't know anything."

"Then tell me," she urged.

"Pamela," he muttered, "was lesson number two."

"Oh, so that's it. A woman disappointed you and now you're sour on the entire gender. That is such a cliché. What happened? Did Pamela decide she couldn't live in Alaska? Was she too much like your mother?"

"It's none of your business."

"You're right, this has nothing to do with me. I have just one more thing to say and then I promise not to mention it again. *Finn Dalton, get over it.*"

Before she could suck in the next breath, Finn's face was two inches away from her own. They were practically nose-to-nose. If Carrie could have backed away, she would have, but with the door pressed against her backside, she had nowhere to move.

Hennessey was on his feet and stood next to Finn, barking madly. Finn ignored him, and so did Carrie.

"I knew Pamela from the time we were teenagers. Or, better yet, I *thought* I knew her. She moved to Seattle and then came back. I loved her, and then I learned that while she was away, she married a soldier who went off to Afghanistan. She didn't care about me. All she wanted was some entertainment while her husband was out of the country. She was playing me. I don't need a woman in my life—got it? Not one of you is worth the heartache. I saw what losing my mother did to my father, and I had a small taste of it myself. I don't need another, so back off. Stay out of my life, understand?"

"Loud and clear." His anger seemed to inhale all the oxygen in the room until the small hairs on the back of Carrie's neck bristled. Her hands were flattened against the door, and when he stepped away it took several seconds before Carrie felt like she could breathe normally again.

He stalked over to his desk on the far side of the cabin as if he couldn't get away from her fast enough.

Carrie bent down to pat Hennessey and reassure him that all was well.

The tension left her shoulders, and she realized she was trembling almost uncontrollably in the aftermath of their confrontation. Despite herself, she felt bad for Finn. Not knowing Pamela or the situation that had led to their breakup, she had to believe it must have been traumatic to Finn.

"My college boyfriend dumped me," Carrie said, and was surprised by how low and shaky her voice sounded.

"And you 'got over it,' right? No big deal." He sat with his back to her, his tone cold. The air seemed to vibrate with tension.

"Actually, no . . . I tried to pretend it was a natural parting of the ways. I was in Chicago, working for the newspaper, and he was back in Seattle. But it hurt," she whispered. "He married a friend of mine six months later, and I was a bridesmaid in their wedding, and I had to pretend it didn't matter."

Finn turned around and looked at her for an extra-long moment, frowning as if to gauge whether she was telling the truth. Carrie held his gaze and didn't flinch before moving into the kitchen, feeling the need to sit down. Her bottom lip trembled slightly, and she bit into it, wanting to disguise how upset she was.

Hennessey sat down by Finn's side, and then after a few minutes walked over to where Carrie sat at the table. She petted his thick fur, trying to think of what to say to ease the tension. They were trapped here together, and she had to do something to make it tolerable.

"We've both been hurt, but it isn't the end of the world."

He snorted.

"Can we put this conversation behind us?"

His back was to her again, and he shrugged.

"Do you play chess?" she asked.

"No."

"Scrabble?"

"No."

What do you play?"

"Solitaire."

"Oh." The hand of truce that Carrie had extended had been solidly slapped.

Several tense moments passed before he exhaled harshly and said, "Do you play cribbage?"

"My grandfather taught me," she responded. If they could find common ground, it would help pass the long hours of being cooped up together until Sawyer arrived. "I'm not much good, but I'd be willing to give it a try if you'd like."

He hesitated and then went into his bedroom and returned with a cribbage board and a deck of cards. Sitting down at the kitchen table across from her, he removed the cards from the box and shuffled.

Carrie was grateful they weren't destined to spend the

entire storm at each other's throats. "Go ahead and deal. How about coffee?"

He nodded.

Finn had dealt the first hand by the time she returned. Carrie looked at her cards, discarded two, and so they started. Luck was with her and she narrowly won the first game. Finn regarded her skeptically. "I thought you said you weren't much good at this?"

"Did I?"

Sipping his coffee, Finn tried to hide his smile, but Carrie saw it and smiled back. "I believe it's my turn to deal."

Keeping his eyes on her, he slid the deck of cards across the table.

Shuffling the cards, Carrie glanced up and smiled ever so sweetly. "Women aren't stupid, you know."

"I never said they were. Heartless, yes, but a few I've happened upon showed meager signs of intelligence."

Carrie suspected he was purposely attempting to bait her. "I'll add *chauvinist* to the long list of words that best describe you, Finn Dalton."

"Better word would be *realist.*"

"Oh, puh-leese." She drawled out the word and laughed despite herself.

Finn did, too, and the surprise of hearing his

amusement caused her to fumble and lose control of the cards, which scattered across the tabletop.

"You should laugh more often," she said, gathering together the deck.

"Really?"

"Yes, really."

His eyes shone, and despite his grizzled appearance, she found him strongly appealing. If he were clean shaven and his hair groomed, he might even be considered handsome. She must have been staring at him because he frowned and barked, "What?"

"Oh, sorry." Carrie quickly looked away and dealt the cards.

"You're staring at me."

"I know."

"Why?"

This question was harder to answer. She couldn't very well admit she found him intriguing, and so she said the first thing that came to mind. "I want to remember what you look like, and I doubt you'd let me take your photo."

He immediately frowned. "For that article you intend to write?"

Instead of answering, she kept dealing the cards and then waited while he cut the deck.

The second game proved they were well matched. Finn won, but not by much.

"Tie-breaker?" he asked.

"Of course," she responded. It surprised her how much she enjoyed this mini–battle of the sexes with him.

After shuffling the cards, he dealt.

"Do you do anything special around the cabin for Christmas?" she asked.

Frowning, he glanced at her above his hand. "It isn't even Thanksgiving yet. Why are you asking about Christmas?"

"I guess it's on my mind. A lot of the stores already have their decorations up."

"You've got to be joking."

"I'm not."

He grumbled some. "I suppose you're the sort of woman who goes all out for Christmas."

"Of course," she said, as she counted out her score. "Although I live alone, I put up a tree, hang garlands, and decorate with holly. What about you?"

He finished counting out his hand. "What about me? If you're digging for more information for that article, you can stop right now."

"I wasn't," she said, groaning. It seemed everything she asked was suspect. "You don't have a Christmas tree?"

"No. Why would I?"

Knowing him, he probably didn't like Christmas at all. "Is it just another day for you and Hennessey?"

"For the most part, yes. I'll sometimes join Sawyer and his family or fly to Fairbanks and spend Christmas Day with friends."

It made Carrie feel better to know he wouldn't be alone unless that was what he chose. "Good."

"Good?" he repeated.

"Yes. I would hate the thought of you spending Christmas alone."

He grinned, as if her comment amused him. "Despite what you think, I enjoy my own company, but I have a real life, too. I live a good part of the time here, but I have a condo . . . elsewhere."

"You do? But how do you support yourself? I mean, before the book."

"I have all the work I want with the state, checking on the pipeline." He grimaced, as if he'd said far more than he meant for her to know. "Forget I said that."

She pantomimed zipping her lips closed. There was far more to Finn than she realized. "Listen, this isn't related to anything I might write, so relax."

They broke for lunch. Finn made sandwiches, which they ate in front of the stove, sitting in the rocking chairs.

A glance out the window told her the wind had died down and the snow had stopped.

"My mother is probably worried about me," she said, checking her cell phone. Thankfully, her battery wasn't dead, but coverage this far north simply wasn't going to happen. "I told her I'd phone, and I haven't. Is there any way I can get word to her?"

"I have a satellite phone, but it isn't cheap."

"I'll be happy to pay whatever the charges are. I won't talk long."

"Having you out of my hair by tomorrow morning would be payment enough."

Carrie frowned. "Ouch. I thought we were getting along so well, too."

Finn chuckled. "We were almost friends until you whipped me in cribbage."

"Ah, men and their fragile egos."

Finn grumbled something she couldn't hear, and then he showed her how to operate the phone by his desk. It took a moment for the line to connect, and when it did, her father answered.

"Dad, it's me. I don't have a lot of time, but I want you to know I'm still in Alaska. Tell Mom I'm doing great and I'll connect with her once I'm back in Chicago."

"Your mother's been concerned. You said you'd call."

"I know, Dad. I'll explain everything when I'm not paying outrageous satellite charges."

"Satellite charges? Where in heaven's name are you?" Her father was the talker in the family.

"Outside of Fairbanks, Alaska." If she said anything more, her dad would have more questions, and then more after that.

"You found him? You found Finn Dalton?"

"Dad, I can't talk now."

"Okay, okay, but I'm going to want a full report once you're back."

"Will do. Reassure Mom that I'm fine and thank Grandpa for teaching me cribbage."

"What's that?"

"Never mind, I'll explain later."

They said their farewells, and Carrie ended the call. When she turned around, she was surprised to find Finn had put on his parka and heavy boots.

"You're going somewhere?" she asked, surprised.

"The wind has died down and the snow has mostly stopped. I won't be gone long." Hennessey was at the door, eager and ready to be on his way.

At the door, Finn hesitated. "You'll be all right for a while by yourself?"

"Of course." It surprised her that he'd asked. Actually,

she welcomed the privacy in order to work on the article. The instant he was out the door, she retrieved her computer. It didn't take her long to organize her thoughts. She'd already gathered more than enough information to write a lengthy piece about him. The rough draft took her the better part of an hour. Feeling good about the piece, which she felt was fair, if not flattering, she tucked her laptop back inside her suitcase, grateful Finn hadn't returned while she'd had it open.

With that out of the way, Carrie soon grew restless and bored, fidgeting, wishing she could talk to Sophie. Had she better planned this trip, she would have brought along her e-reader.

Finding little with which to entertain herself, Carrie took out the paper tablet she had with her, found a pair of scissors, and went about cutting large snowflakes. With the sewing kit at the bottom of her purse, she took thread, stood barefoot on a chair, and suspended the flakes from the ceiling until the entire cabin looked like a magical winter wonderland.

More than likely Finn wouldn't appreciate her effort toward Christmas decorations; however, she wasn't going to let that stop her. Other than keeping her occupied, she hoped this would amuse him.

She was standing on the chair in the middle of the

cabin, stretching her arms above her head, when the door unexpectedly opened and Finn and Hennessey stepped inside.

"What the . . ."

Startled, Carrie lost her balance, and with arms flailing at her sides, she started to topple from her perch on the chair. Seeing her predicament, Finn reacted quickly and instinctively, catching her in midair. Carrie issued a small, breathless gasp as her body was pressed hard against his.

For one wild moment all they did was stare at each other. Her pulse raced, and his eyes went directly to her throat as if he could see her reaction. He didn't release her, and she realized she was glad to be in his arms. It wasn't a comfortable feeling.

His gaze traveled from the throbbing pulse in her neck to her lips, and Carrie's mouth went dry as his eyes held hers. When did this happen? Another question quickly followed the first—what were they going to do about it? Carrie knew what she wanted. She closed her eyes, expecting, hoping that Finn would kiss her.

He didn't.

Gradually he released her, setting her feet down on solid ground. Then he stepped back as though having her this close had burned his senses.

"What is this?" he asked, his voice ragged, demanding. He hardly sounded like himself.

"What?" Carrie's own senses became jumbled. Confused. She wasn't sure what he meant. It sounded as if he was asking about this sudden arc of awareness that vibrated between them. "I . . ."

"This!" He pointed at the ceiling.

"Oh, that," she said, feeling foolish, embarrassed, and relieved. "I thought I'd add a bit of holiday spirit to your cabin."

He frowned.

"I can take it down if you want."

His response was a soft snort. "And risk you breaking your fool neck a second time? Leave it."

"I think it looks great."

"You would."

"And you don't?" she pressed.

He didn't bother to answer, but instead announced, "I'll put a roast on for dinner." She stood by while he put together meat, carrots, and onions in a cast-iron pot and placed it in the oven.

"What can I do?" she asked, looking to help.

"You can peel potatoes if you want."

"I want."

They both seemed eager to put that sensual

awkwardness behind them. It was important, she supposed, to ignore the awareness that sprang up so unexpectedly. Finn seemed as determined as she was to pretend it had never happened. Carrie was more than eager to do so, seeing that she'd practically begged him to kiss her. Just thinking about it mortified her. She didn't know what she'd been thinking, which explained it, because clearly she hadn't been thinking. Instead, she'd been feeling, and that was dangerous to them both.

Within a couple of hours the scent of the roast filled the cabin. As she set the table for dinner, Finn disappeared for a couple minutes and returned with a bottle of red wine.

"Do you like wine?" he asked.

"Yes, very much."

He set the wine bottle in the middle of the table.

"Are we celebrating?" she asked, teasing him.

"Yes. Sawyer will collect you come morning."

"Of course. How could I have forgotten?" she said. "And you'll be more than ready to see me go."

To her surprise, he didn't immediately respond.

When dinner was ready, they sat down across from each other, the roast and assorted vegetables on a platter between them. Finn opened the wine bottle and poured them each a glass.

"What shall we toast?" she asked, pressing the brim of her glass against his.

"To cribbage," he suggested. "And I demand a rematch after dinner."

"To cribbage," she echoed, and smiled.

Their eyes held for an extra-long moment, and her stomach was filled with butterflies as she realized that this heightened awareness of each other hadn't gone away. If anything, it was stronger, and was growing more so each moment. Although they both tried to ignore what was happening, it was still there, as real and as profound as when he'd caught her and kept her from falling to the floor.

They sipped the wine while their gazes held. Deliberately, Carrie looked away. She needed to remind herself that the sole reason she was in Alaska was for an interview. After spending more than twenty-four hours with Finn, she had what she needed. And as soon as the article was published, Finn Dalton would want nothing more to do with her.

# Chapter 6

This wasn't working, Finn realized. When Carrie showed up unexpectedly, he'd been determined to freeze her out. She might have found him, but she wasn't getting one iota of information out of him for that blasted article she intended to write. He would say as little as possible, speak in monosyllables, and be rid of her the instant the weather cleared.

And yet within the span of twenty-four hours she knew more about him than he ever intended. Only a few of his friends knew about his involvement with Pamela. If divulging personal information wasn't bad enough, he'd been keenly tempted to take her in his arms and kiss her. The urge had been so strong that he'd had to leave the cabin. Then, upon his return, he'd found her standing on a chair and she'd fallen directly into his arms. He'd like to think she planned this, but her reactions said otherwise. He'd caught her, and she'd looked up at him with those baby blues of hers, practically begging him to do the very thing he wanted to most. It felt as if he was about to go down for the third time before he gathered the strength to pull away. Not that it was easy. Finn liked to think of himself as disciplined and in control of his emotions. With Carrie, every bit of self-preservation flew out the proverbial window. He didn't like it one bit.

What he needed, Finn decided, was a distraction. He figured if they could play cards, that would keep him sane until he was well rid of her. Then he'd come up with the bright idea of opening a bottle of wine. What *was* he thinking? If he found her beautiful before dinner, she was all the more so during. Stunning, breathtakingly beautiful, and for the life of him he couldn't keep his eyes off her.

He wanted to blame the wine, but she'd intoxicated him with little more than a smile. This was bad, and every minute he spent with her made it worse. Before he knew how it happened, he'd lowered his guard.

"Are you surprised?" she'd asked him. "You know, by how successful the book has been?"

He nodded. It baffled him even now. His editor routinely updated him on sales and his position on the *New York Times* bestseller list. "I've been told it's a publishing sensation."

"It is. Finn, thousands and thousands of people are reading and loving your stories about Alaska. What ever made you think to write it?"

He smiled and leaned back, far more comfortable with her than he should have been. Before he knew it, he was telling her the story. "It was just one of those things. I read an article about the problems with kids having sedentary lives, obsessed with video games and television, and was astonished. While I was growing up, every day was an adventure. I thought if I wrote about some of my own experiences it might inspire kids and adults to step outside their front door and look at nature in an entirely different way."

Carrie's eyes brightened and Finn couldn't have looked away from her if someone had offered him gold ingots.

"Did you know," Carrie said, her smile warm and alive, "there are whole groups that are springing up across the country for organized hikes and other outdoor activities that your book inspired? This would never have happened if it hadn't been for your book. I hope you realize what a strong influence *Alone* has been."

He had heard about such groups, and it pleased him immensely.

The bottom line, Finn realized, was that he needed to keep his trap shut.

The problem was how comfortable he felt with Carrie. Hardly trying, she got him talking. He wasn't sure what it was about her; maybe it was the pain that radiated from her when she spoke of her college sweetheart. At first he assumed she'd made up the story in order to gain his trust. But the hurt he saw in her couldn't be fabricated. No one was that good an actress.

All Finn could hope was that Sawyer didn't get delayed come morning. There was still a chance that Finn might come out of this fiasco unscathed.

Carrie and Finn worked together washing and drying the dinner dishes. Although she pretended not to notice, he kept a careful watch on her. At one point she almost said she had no intention of stealing his silverware.

Dinner had been pleasant enough. The roast had been cooked to perfection, tender and succulent, and the vegetables were a wonderful complement. They'd chatted amicably during the meal, and Carrie was surprised how easy it was to talk to Finn. Without her prompting, he'd started to talk about the book, which shocked her. When he abruptly stopped, she realized he'd said far more than he'd ever intended.

"I like you, Finn," she said as they claimed the chairs by the fire.

"Excuse me?" He arched one thick brow as though questioning her.

"With few exceptions, I've enjoyed spending this time with you."

"Really?" Her announcement appeared to amuse him. He leaned back in his chair and crossed his arms as though he expected her to elaborate.

She rocked a bit before answering. "I'm not going to feed your ego."

"Come on. Why not?"

Carrie had trouble holding back a smile "Okay, fine," she said, "you're so authentic. You are who you are and you aren't willing to apologize for it. I like that."

Actually, she was strongly attracted to the fact that Finn was a man's man, but she wasn't willing to admit it. His strength didn't come from working out in some gym but from living life.

She found he was staring at her, and so she continued,

"Covering the society page the way I do, you can't imagine how many men . . . and women I meet who only care about money, appearances, superficial things. Oh, don't get me started, but you . . . you're a refreshing change."

"I'm highly intelligent," he added.

She laughed. "And humble, too, I see."

"Touché." He chuckled and then asked, "What about good-looking?"

"I don't feel qualified to answer that," she said, and cocked her head from one side to the other as though assessing his looks.

"Why not?" he challenged.

She flexed her fingers over her own cheeks. "It's hard to tell with your entire face covered with that beard."

"True, but you should be able to take my word for it. Besides, beards are a necessity here in Alaska."

"Someone should have told me and I would have grown one," she joked.

He smiled back, and it seemed like their gazes caught and held for an extra-long moment. In order to break the spell, she looked away and added, "You're a good conversationalist."

He frowned at her comment. "Too good."

Their conversation continued for another hour. Carrie discovered that they had a surprising amount in common and agreed on a number of issues; they both loved reading thrillers and were big football fans, especially of the Seattle Seahawks. On others, they were diametrically opposed, the foremost being politics. What struck her, what she found devastatingly attractive about him, was the fact that he could laugh at himself and about Alaska. Finn possessed a wonderful dry wit. When she asked him about the rumor that Alaska was full of bachelors, he replied, "You know what they say about Alaska, don't you? It's where the men are men, and so are the women."

Carrie tried unsuccessfully to hide her laugh, nearly choking with the effort. Once she composed herself she recited something she'd read on a T-shirt. "I heard that if a woman is looking for a husband in Alaska, her odds are good but the goods are odd."

Finn laughed in return, and then it happened again. Their gazes caught and held for what seemed like an eternity, as neither one of them was keen to break the contact.

Carrie hadn't been joking; she enjoyed Finn's company. The more she got to know him, the stronger her feelings became. Before long, they'd finished off the bottle of wine. Then Finn suggested a rematch of their cribbage game.

"Only this time whoever wins the match gets the bed tonight," he suggested.

Carrie didn't need to think twice about this wager. "You're on." The only decent sleep she'd had the night before had been in Finn's bed, and that had been right before morning. She remembered wrapping herself up in the warm quilts, surrounded by the scent of Finn. The sofa had been lumpy, and half the night she'd shivered with cold. It'd been an uncomfortable experience. The one bonus was having Hennessey with her.

Once again Finn brought out the cribbage board and the cards, and they sat down across from each other as they had before. They cut the cards, and Finn won for the deal. As he shuffled the deck, he made light conversation, almost as if he was looking to distract her.

"You said you work for the *Chicago Herald*?"

"Yeah." She caught the cards as he dealt them to her. "The society page, like I said earlier."

Finn arched his brows.

"I'm fortunate to have a job with such a prestigious newspaper, but quite honestly, Finn, this isn't the type of writing I want to do." The thought of returning to Chicago and immediately being thrust into a series of parties and other social events filled her with dread.

"So that's the reason you went to such desperate lengths to find me."

"Right. An article on you would change everything for me." She glanced up hopefully, but his expression remained blank. He didn't need to tell her his feelings on the matter; they'd already been well stated. But she would write the article. The nearly thirty-six hours she'd spent in his company had proved he was everything he'd claimed in his book and more.

Finn laid down his first card, and she immediately added her own.

Carrie would like to think that it was because she was distracted by their conversation that she handily lost the first game.

"No fair," she muttered.

"Are you suggesting I cheated?" he asked, and seemed to enjoy her loss far too much.

"No, but you distracted me, got me thinking about . . . work."

"That's a convenient excuse, and you know it. The fact is I played a superior game."

"Sure you did," she muttered sarcastically, and reached for the deck. "We're playing for the match, remember."

"Why don't you rest your brain for a few minutes?" Finn suggested, his voice dripping with pretend sympathy. He rose from the table and came to stand behind her, and placed his hands on her shoulders. He rubbed and kneaded the knotted flesh as shivers of awareness shot down her spine. Giving in to his touch, Carrie closed her eyes with a sigh and let her head drop forward. This was divine. It might have been her imagination, but for just an instant she thought she felt his breath against the side of her neck as if he'd bent over to kiss it. His touch was so light, so tender, that it could well have been wishful thinking. From everything Finn had said, he was more than eager to be rid of her.

"What I need," she said, scooting back her chair, anxious to break this trance that had come over her, "is some fresh air." As it was, the room seemed overwhelmingly stuffy. The storm was over, and the night appeared relatively peaceful.

Handing Carrie her coat, Finn walked her to the front door. When she stepped outside, her arms immediately went about her middle as her gaze went to the star-filled heavens. In all her life, Carrie had never seen so many stars. Thousands upon thousands of pinpricks of twinkling light dotted the sky, mesmerizing her.

"Oh, my," she whispered, caught up in the magic of the moment. "This is unbelievable."

Finn came to stand behind her, his hands on her shoulders. "I never grow tired of this view," he whispered.

"No wonder. It's incredible. Awesome. Breathtaking."

"Now look north." He turned her halfway around so that she faced the arctic.

Carrie gasped. The sky was filled with wave upon wave of color—gold, bronze, and lavender arced across the night sky. "Is that the . . . aurora borealis?"

"You've never seen it before?"

"No. Of course, I've heard about it, but I had no idea it was this beautiful, this dramatic." Just watching the northern lights dance their seductive ballet chased off the chill of the frigid night. Then Carrie realized the source of this toasty feeling was Finn's arms, which surrounded her. He'd tucked his warm body close to hers, warding off the frigid night air.

"Close your eyes," he suggested, his head close to hers.

She did as he requested.

"Do you hear anything?" His breath was warm against her ear.

"Yes," she whispered. "A crackling sound."

"That's the northern lights. Not everyone can hear them."

"Can you?" she asked, barely getting the words out. Having him this close took her breath away.

"Yes." His lips nuzzled her neck, and Carrie sighed audibly.

At the same moment, they both seemed to become aware of the close proximity they shared, knit together, as it were. Without a word, Finn snatched his arms away and returned to the house.

Carrie followed a moment later. Finn was already sitting at the table by the time she closed and latched the door.

"Is your brain working now?" he asked, and cleared his throat, busying himself with shuffling the cards.

"Ah, sure." Her breath trembled slightly, and she hoped that if Finn noticed he wouldn't comment.

"I don't think I've ever seen anything more beautiful," she whispered.

"Me neither," Finn added.

Her mind swirled with the sights and sounds of the innate beauty of Alaska. Inhaling a deep breath, she glanced up to find Finn studying her. She wanted to thank him for sharing his home and his life with her for the past two days. The words were on the tip of her tongue, but she doubted she could murmur a single word without tears leaking from her eyes. These last few minutes had felt almost spiritual, as if she'd been standing in a church and singing hymns of praise.

As best she could, Carrie returned to the game, doing her utmost to pretend nothing out of the ordinary had happened and at the same moment acutely aware that it had.

As luck would have it, she won the second game, but it was no thanks to her skilled card sense. The air between them sizzled and arced much like the northern lights, even as they both chose to ignore it. Perhaps that was for the best, as she would be flying out at first light. An immediate sense of regret filled her. In an amazingly short amount of time, Alaska had won her over, and Finn had, too.

The last cribbage game was close, but in the end Finn won. Little wonder, really, as Carrie's mind was not on the game. She didn't know how she was going to say good-bye when she had the distinct feeling she would be leaving her heart behind.

Finn seemed surprised that he managed to pull out a win. Carrie sighed as she set her cards down and pulled the pegs from the board. She wasn't looking forward to another miserable night on the sofa, but, all things considered, a little discomfort was a small price to pay.

Finn seemed to read her lack of communication as disappointment. "You can have the bed," he told her.

"No. You won," she said much too cheerfully, overcompensating. "I'm the intruder here, remember?" Hennessey would lie at her feet, and he'd keep her company during the night. It wouldn't be so bad, and if she was fortunate enough to catch the flight back to Seattle and then make a quick connection to Chicago, she could sleep on the plane.

Finn reached for the cards and placed them back inside the box.

"I realize having me as your houseguest wasn't what you wanted," she said. "You've been more than gracious, and I want to thank you for putting up with me."

He shrugged, giving the impression it wasn't a big deal. "You aren't so bad."

"Contrary to popular opinion, you aren't, either."

He cracked a smile. "Your opinion?"

"Well," she said, "we didn't exactly start off on the right foot."

"True," he acknowledged.

"Are you still upset with Sawyer?"

He gave the question some consideration before answering. "I'll settle up with him later."

"Don't be too hard on him," Carrie pleaded. "He's a good friend to you."

"He is," Finn agreed.

A short while later Finn announced it was time to call it a night. Despite the fact that it was relatively early, Carrie was tired. He offered her privacy so she could wash up and change clothes. While she was getting ready for bed, Finn contacted Sawyer. She heard the two men talking over the ham radio but was able to make out only half of what was being said.

When she reappeared, Finn said, "Sawyer will arrive early. He'll see you to the terminal and make sure you have a seat on the next available flight out of Fairbanks to Seattle."

"But how ..." This was the one drawback to her plan. She'd arrived in Alaska, and not knowing when to book her return ticket, she'd left it open. Now she would need to purchase a last-minute ticket back to Chicago at a greatly inflated price. Because of cutbacks with the airlines, almost every plane she'd flown on lately had been packed with passengers like sardines in a can. All she could hope was that there would be a seat available.

"Sawyer works with the airlines. They owe him a favor. Don't worry—it's all being taken care of."

Although the two friends seemed to have reached an

understanding, it appeared Finn was still eager to send her on her way. She had to believe he'd experienced the same tenderness and awareness she had. The electricity between them was powerful enough to light up a city block. Surely he felt it, too. Like her, it probably made him uncomfortable, and the best way he could deal with it was to send her packing.

Carrie could find no way of telling him that she wouldn't mind spending a few more days. That was crazy thinking on her part, but she couldn't shake this reluctance to leave. It seemed they were just beginning to come to an understanding, a willingness to explore whatever it was that was happening between them.

"Time for lights out," Finn said, and his voice sounded odd, regretful.

"Right." How she wished she knew what he was thinking.

He brought out the blankets and pillow for her. Carrie held out her arms to take the load, but he hesitated. "You're sure about this? I don't mind taking the sofa tonight."

"That's generous, but a deal is a deal."

"Okay, your choice."

"Right again."

He built up the fire and then returned to the bedroom.

Carrie made her bed, sat on the sofa, and wrapped her arms around her bent knees.

To her surprise, Finn hadn't mentioned her article again. She half expected him to argue his case, demand that she honor his privacy. Instead, he'd avoided the subject entirely. He hadn't sought out this notoriety, even if he had written one of the most intriguing and interesting books of the year. Although there was so much more she wanted to know about him, it seemed wrong to press the point. As far as she was concerned, the article was fast becoming secondary to everything else.

Eventually Carrie fell asleep, her mind full of Finn, the man she was just beginning to know and wished to know much better. He wasn't like anyone she'd ever met, which intrigued her all the more. The businessmen and the community leaders she met at social functions were as different as night and day from a man like Finn, and yet she was strongly attracted to him. She found him more appealing than anyone she'd recently dated, that was for sure.

For the last few months she'd gone out with Dave Schneider a number of times. It wasn't anywhere close to serious. She enjoyed his company, but as a salesman, he traveled frequently, and their schedules didn't often mesh. While she had ample opportunities to date, the men she usually met were too slick, too polished, too caught up in themselves and their careers to appeal to her. She couldn't see making a life with anyone in her current social network.

At some point during the night, Carrie stirred awake to find Finn kneeling over her. Leaning up on one elbow, she rubbed the sleep from her eyes. "Is it morning already?" she asked. A sense of dread filled her. She didn't want to leave—not yet. Not so soon.

He shook his head. "Take the bed. I can't sleep."

She wanted to argue but could see it would do her no good. Tossing aside the blanket, she started to get up but instead Finn effortlessly lifted her into his arms and carried her into his bedroom.

He pressed her down on the feather mattress and, leaning forward, kissed her brow. "Sleep tight," he whispered.

Reaching up, she cupped the side of his face, his beard prickling her palm, and she smiled at him softly, silently wishing that he would kiss her for real. She moistened her lips, inviting him to take what she offered. Surely he could read the longing in her eyes; surely he knew what she wanted. Instead, he reluctantly straightened and left the room.

Carrie tried but found she was unable to fall back to sleep. Apparently, Finn wasn't having much luck, either, because she could hear him moving about the outer room as if he was as restless as she was.

Seeking a comfortable position, Carrie tried sleeping on one side, then the other, and finally lay on her back, staring up at the ceiling. His room had a window, and after what seemed like an eternity, she tossed the thick covers away and climbed out of bed. Her feet made no sound as she walked over to the window and pushed the curtain to one side. Staring into the night, she looked up at the heavens.

Once more she was struck by the brilliant dark sky with countless stars. The moon was full and lit up the frozen lake like stage lighting. No wonder Finn loved Alaska. This was a magical place, beautiful and uncomplicated, so far removed from the craziness of city life.

After a while she returned to the main room to find Finn sitting at his desk. Right away he heard her and whirled around in his chair. He seemed surprised to find her awake.

"I couldn't sleep, either," she confessed.

He immediately closed the document on his computer, as if he didn't want her to see what he was writing.

"Another book?" she dared to ask.

"If I admit it, will you put that in the article?" The question was more of an accusation.

"I . . . I don't know."

He closed the lid to the laptop.

"If you're writing a sequel, I can tell you your readers will be more than thrilled."

He ignored the comment and glanced at his wrist. "Sawyer should be here within the hour."

"Already?" It seemed far too soon. She wasn't eager to leave. Finn's father's wedding band remained in her jeans pocket, and she thought to simply leave it in the cabin for him to find once she was gone. However, seeing his reaction to it earlier prompted her to keep it for now. She'd return the gold ring to his mother at Christmas.

Sure enough, within the hour the sound of an approaching aircraft filled the house. The noise seemed to multiply, stirring up the atmosphere inside the cabin, building anticipation.

"That must be Sawyer," Finn said.

Carrie nodded. Dragging her carry-on to the door, she checked the cabin to be sure she hadn't left anything behind.

Finn stood in the kitchen sipping coffee, as if, in these final moments, he wanted to keep as much distance between them as possible.

Hennessey barked, and rushed to the door, wanting out. Finn opened it just as the float plane bounced against the solid ice and skidded for several feet in the surrounding moonlight.

"The trip out here was my first experience in a single-engine plane," she said, more to fill the silence than to make a statement.

Without commenting, Finn reached for her suitcase and carried it outside. Carrie followed, a lump in her throat. That she should get all emotional over this farewell was an embarrassment. She was determined not to let Finn see how discombobulated she felt. It was ridiculous. She barely knew this man. He'd let it be known she was a nuisance and considered himself well rid of her.

By the time she reached the plane, Finn had the passenger door open and her suitcase stored inside. He exchanged a few short sentences with Sawyer, but she couldn't hear what he said over the roar of the engine.

Carrie made sure she had a smile in place when he turned to face her. She hadn't thought what her last words to him would be, and so she said what came instinctively.

"Thank you for everything."

Cupping her shoulders, Finn looked down on her, his

dark eyes as intense as she could ever remember seeing them.

She met his gaze, wanting to tell him without words how much the last two days had meant to her, and how impressed she was with the man he was. She longed to thank him for opening her eyes to what it was to be with a man who was passionate about life and who had shared that passion through stories of life in Alaska.

Staring down at her, his hands tightened. He murmured something she didn't understand, and then he pulled her close as if he couldn't help himself and lowered his mouth to hers.

Carrie gave a small cry of welcome and gratitude and clung to him. Finn's hands cupped her face as he tilted her head to receive his kiss, which felt urgent and needy, needs that mirrored her own.

For a moment the sheer wonder of it nearly caused Carrie's knees to collapse from under her. This was exactly what she wanted, what she'd hoped would happen. And his kiss was everything she could have imagined. More. Without fully being aware of what she was doing, Carrie locked her arms around his neck and kissed him back, wanting to return everything that he had given her.

After a long moment, Finn gradually released her

from the kiss, but he still hugged her close and tight against him, half lifting her from the frozen lakebed.

"Good-bye, Finn," she whispered close to his ear.

He kissed her neck and then whispered back, "Good-bye."

She started to climb into the airplane but Finn stopped her by gripping hold of her hand. He looked deep into her eyes as if to gauge her reaction, and then leaned forward and said, "Carrie?"

"Yes?" Her heart was in her eyes. Could it be possible that he would ask her to stay? Did it seem as wrong to him as it did to her that they should part now? Surely he felt the very things she did.

Leaning in close, he kissed her one last time and then said, "Don't write the article."

# Chapter 7

The wheels of the Boeing 737 bounced against the O'Hare tarmac as the plane landed safely, jolting Carrie out of a light slumber. She hadn't slept as much on the long flight back to Chicago as she'd hoped, which wasn't surprising. She glanced at her watch and realized she was still on Alaska time.

Finn time.

He'd asked her not to write the article. Surely he understood what that meant. She'd explained to him what this piece could do for her career. It would change everything for her. As she boarded the flight in Seattle, Carrie was forced to ask herself if invading his privacy was worth the cost. Perhaps the answer should seem obvious, but she still wasn't sure what she would do.

The temptation to ignore his request was strong. In every likelihood she might never see or hear from the elusive Finn Dalton again. Surely he understood how unreasonable he was being, how selfish, but then . . . wasn't she being selfish, too?

Monday morning, after sleeping on it, Carrie had her answer. She wouldn't finish her story about Finn Dalton. No matter what happened or didn't happen between them, it wouldn't be worth the price. Every woman Finn had ever known had betrayed him, and she was determined not to be one of them. If there was a chance he would ever learn to trust and love again, then the path would start with her. It meant sacrifice on her end, but all she could do was hope that someday he would thank her. Someone else was sure to find him, one day, and the author of *Alone* would be exposed to the world, but she wouldn't be the reporter who did it.

Carrie wasn't at her desk two minutes before Sophie showed up, nearly bouncing with energy and excitement. "Well?" she asked expectantly. "How'd it go?"

Glancing up at her friend, Carrie made sure her face didn't give anything away. "Go?" she repeated, as though she didn't understand the question.

"Did you find him?"

"You mean Finn Dalton?" Carrie's mind scrambled with ways of answering without telling an outright lie. "It was a needle-in-a-haystack idea. I must have been out of my mind to think I could jet off to Alaska and stumble upon the one man half the world is dying to read about."

"Yeah, but did you find him?"

Leave it to Sophie to press the point. "Honestly, would I be sitting here so glum if I had?" She was in a blue funk, but it was due to other reasons. Lack of sleep, for one; missing Finn, for another. Really missing Finn. Thinking back on their final minutes together, there'd been a hundred things she wished she'd said, and she hadn't managed to get out even one coherent thought. Well, other than a generic "thank you for everything." And "good-bye." How lame was that! Nor had she said good-bye to Hennessey.

Sawyer had certainly been curious, drilling her with questions much in the same way Sophie was just now.

"Seems like you two got along just fine," the bush pilot had commented.

"Not at first."

He'd chuckled. "I can well imagine. You won him over, though, I see."

"Did I?" she asked Sawyer. She might never know the answer to that.

"I thought for sure you had a chance," Sophie said, dragging Carrie back into the dreary present. Monday mornings were bad enough, but this Monday was even worse, especially on only a few hours' rest.

Carrie couldn't stop thinking about Finn, couldn't stop dreaming about him. If any two people were dissimilar, it was them, and yet the attraction had been magnetic and powerful. Now that she was gone, she wondered if she remained on his mind the way he did on hers.

"How disappointing for you," Sophie said, her eyes wide with sympathy.

"I really thought I had a line on him, too," Carrie confessed. Only she was the one who'd fallen—hook, line, and sinker.

"You located his mother, though, right?" Sophie leaned against the side of Carrie's desk and crossed her arms.

"Yes, and that got me really excited, but mother and son have been estranged since Finn was ten years old. All she really knew was that he was living in Alaska, and that it was close to Fairbanks. Unfortunately, her directions were too vague to help."

"What happened when you got to Fairbanks?" Sophie hopped up onto the corner of Carrie's desk as though she intended to stay awhile.

"Well, for one thing, I discovered I wasn't the only reporter who'd arrived out of the blue searching for the elusive Finn Dalton."

"Who did you ask?"

"Bush pilots. From what I heard, Finn is a pilot himself." Carrie had learned from Sawyer on their flight back that Finn owned a plane, which was currently in Fairbanks for a routine maintenance check.

"How do you know that?"

"Word of mouth."

"Whose word?"

"Does it matter?" Carrie was growing irritated with Sophie's questions. In retrospect, she wished she hadn't said anything. At the time, she'd been too excited to keep the information to herself.

"Did any of those pilots give you anything you could use?" Sophie seemed obsessed with this, and Carrie was finding it difficult to give her friend ambiguous answers.

"Don't you have work to do?" Carrie asked instead.

"Yes, but it seems to me the bush pilots must know Finn and would tell you something, anything."

"Wrong. Finn has very loyal friends."

"You could have bribed them; did you think of that?"

"Sophie, please, it's my first day back and I've got a ton of stuff to catch up on."

"All right, all right. I just hope you aren't too disappointed."

She sighed. "I'm not. I gave finding him my best shot and turned up empty. I can't do anything more than that."

"So you're going to give up just like that?" Sophie appeared stunned. "That doesn't sound like you at all. When you left Chicago, you had that bloodhound look in your eyes, your nose to the ground with a determination to go above and beyond to find this guy. Now it seems like you hardly care at all."

"Maybe that's because I'm looking to keep the job I already have. Now, please leave me alone, would you?" Carrie was fast losing her patience. Sophie made it nearly impossible to continue this charade.

"It's not like you to be so secretive." Sophie leaped off the desk and stood staring at Carrie as though she no longer recognized her friend. Then she sadly shook her head and returned to her own cubicle.

The tension between Carrie's shoulder blades gradually relaxed. She'd passed the first test—at least she hoped she had. Now all she had to do was concentrate on putting her energy into the society page and making the most of her current position. She couldn't help being disappointed. When it came to Finn, she'd made her decision, and right or wrong, she was sticking to it. She cared too much to betray him.

Her morning was completely eaten up by answering emails. She worked straight through lunch and grabbed coffee and a muffin around two. Her phone rang just as she sat back down at her desk. She reached for her extension with one hand and her coffee with the other.

"Carrie Slayton."

"Hi." The lone word sounded as if it had come from the moon.

Carrie nearly came out of her chair. It was Finn. "What are you doing calling me here?" she whispered in a near panic. She leaned halfway over her desk and kept her voice as low as possible.

"I wanted to see if you got back okay."

"I did." Carrie cupped her hand over the phone's mouthpiece. "You shouldn't phone me here; it's dangerous."

"Do you want me to phone you?"

"Yes, oh, yes." She didn't bother to hide her enthusiasm. The sound of his voice washed over her, warming her, filling her with a rush of joy.

"Give me your cell number, then," he suggested.

She rattled it off and had him repeat it to be sure he'd written it down correctly. "Are you on the satellite phone?" she asked, her heart hammering wildly.

"Yes."

"I thought you said it was expensive."

"Very."

She smiled and closed her eyes at the happiness that settled over her. "Does that mean you miss me?"

He grumbled a phrase she didn't understand. "It must," he muttered. "Does that make you happy?"

"Very."

He chuckled. "Can I call you tonight?"

"Yes," she said automatically, then realized she was covering an art gallery opening. "No, sorry. I've got an assignment this evening."

"Will there be lots of men around?"

"Tons."

He grumbled again in the same vague way he had earlier.

"Are you jealous?"

"Should I be?"

Carrie smiled. "That depends. If you're intimidated by clean-shaven, handsome men in slick black suits who hardly know which end of a car has the gas tank, then be my guest."

"Guess I'm in the clear after all."

"I'd say so," she agreed.

"What time will you be home?"

Carrie wished she could give him a definite time. "Can't say. Hopefully before eleven, but I can never predict how long these events will last."

"Which is one reason you dislike this society-page reporting as much as you do."

"You could say that." She clung to the phone, not wanting to end the call, even if the cost was exorbitant. "How did you get my number?"

"Not much of an investigative reporter if you need to ask that. I called the newspaper and asked to be connected to the society-page editor."

"Of course." Plainly, she wasn't thinking clearly. It came to her then the real reason behind his call. As much as she wanted to believe it was because he couldn't live without hearing the sound of her voice, she knew otherwise. "You called because you want to know if I've reached a decision, didn't you?"

He didn't answer right away. "It's more than that, I . . ."

"I know what I'm going to do."

The line went still and silent. "And what did you decide?"

"Rest easy, Dr. Livingston, your secrets are safe with me."

"Doctor who?"

"Livingston. All the world was on a search to find him, too, if you remember."

"Oh, right."

"You could email me."

"What's your email address?"

She gave him her private email address, unwilling to risk someone from the office stumbling upon their communication.

"I should go," he said.

"I know." As much as she wanted to talk to him, someone might overhear and connect the dots. Lowering her voice, she added, "Call me tonight, okay?" It probably wasn't smart to let him know how eager she was to hear from him again, but she couldn't stop herself. She was falling for this guy. And falling hard.

"Okay. Eleven your time, eight mine."

"Perfect." No matter what, she intended to leave the art show in plenty of time to be home for Finn's call.

Somehow Carrie got through the evening, smiling at all the right times, taking down names, and making the most of the event for the following day's newspaper. Harry, the staff photographer, glanced her way suspiciously a couple of times.

"What's up?" he asked, as they hurriedly walked toward the parking garage. She still had to write the story and get it in before the press deadline.

"What do you mean?" She played innocent, although she was practically trotting in her eagerness to escape.

"I've never seen you in such an all-fired hurry like this. You meeting someone later?"

"No," she said, in complete honesty.

Harry shrugged. "Whatever you say."

Carrie arrived back at her condo fifteen minutes early. She kicked off her shoes, wiggled out of her dress, shimmied out of her pantyhose, and grabbed her warmest pjs. She tossed back the covers to her bed, climbed in, and sat cross-legged with her cell phone clasped in her hand, waiting for Finn's call.

Twice she caught herself falling asleep, so when the phone rang, it surprised her and she nearly dropped it.

"Hi," she said, and knew she sounded breathless. "You're right on time."

"Hi, yourself."

Right away she noticed that the call had a different sound to it. "Where are you?" she asked.

"Fairbanks. I figured it would make talking to you a whole lot more convenient."

"That explains why you sound as if you're in the next room instead of outer space."

"The first call did come from outer space."

She grinned. "Exactly."

"So how did the art show opening go?"

"Harry was suspicious."

"Who's Harry?"

He sounded worried, which thrilled her. "The staff photographer, who's at least fifty and has a half-dozen kids."

"What do you mean he was suspicious?"

This was a bit more difficult to explain. "He could tell I couldn't wait to get out of the show; I kept glancing at my watch."

"Maybe it would be better if we emailed."

She thought about that for a moment. "You're probably right."

"We won't need to worry about the time difference, then."

"Agreed."

"You sound reluctant. Is there a reason?"

To this point, she hadn't done a decent job of hiding her feelings toward him, so now probably wasn't a good time to start. "I like hearing the sound of your voice."

He didn't say anything for a moment. "I like hearing your voice, too. I have something for you."

"What?" Her curiosity was instantly piqued.

"It's a surprise."

"A gift?"

"I wouldn't exactly call it that . . . it's something I'd like you to have. I've already sent it off. I shipped it overnight, so you should have it tomorrow or Wednesday at the latest."

"Oh, Finn, I can't imagine what it could be." Her mind toyed with several possibilities. She'd seen a number of items on the shelves in his cabin that interested her. A beautiful piece of scrimshaw was the first thing that came to mind, and another was a small wood carving. During her short visit she hadn't seen evidence that he carved wood, but it seemed like something that would interest him.

They spoke for a full hour, until Carrie found it impossible to smother her yawns any longer.

"You're exhausted," he whispered. "I need to let you go."

"No, just a few minutes longer," she pleaded, yawning again.

"Carrie, you're practically falling asleep while on the phone. I'll email you so when you wake up there'll be a message waiting for you."

"Promise?"

"Promise."

She smiled sleepily and admitted, "I didn't sleep very well the last couple of nights."

"Me neither."

"I will tonight."

"So will I. Sweet dreams," he whispered.

They would be sweet because they would be filled with Finn.

Six and a half hours later Carrie woke to the sound of her bedside alarm, feeling rested. Stretching her arms above her head, she arched her back and smiled contentedly. Then, remembering Finn's promise, she hurried out of bed and brewed a single cup of coffee while she logged on to her computer. Sure enough, Finn had sent her an email that included the tracking number for the surprise he had mailed her.

Later that same afternoon, a midsize box was delivered to her desk. Carrie knew immediately that it was from Finn.

"What's that?" Sophie asked, coming out of her cubicle.

"I don't know." She lifted the box and carefully shook it. That didn't tell her anything, though.

"Who's it from?"

Carrie pretended to read the return address. "A friend," she said nonchalantly.

"Male or female?"

"Male. Like I said, a friend."

"Well, for heaven's sake, don't keep me in suspense. Open it."

Carrie was more than curious herself. She tore open the box to find it filled with those irritating packing peanuts. She had to dig deep into the box before she found her treasure.

When she pulled it free, Sophie immediately started to laugh. "Is this someone's idea of a joke?" she asked.

Carrie didn't have an answer. This was quite possibly the very last thing she would even have guessed that Finn could possibly mail her.

Inside the box, carefully packaged and protected with packing peanuts, was an antique toaster.

# *Chapter 8*

From: girlygirl@chicago.com
Sent: November 13, 2013
To: alaskaman@fairbankscable.com
Subject: A toaster?

Finn,
You spent a fortune to mail me a toaster? My friend
Sophie thinks it's some silly joke, but I know you, and
this isn't a joke. What's the story?
  Carrie


From: alaskaman@fairbankscable.com

Sent: November 13, 2013
To: girlygirl@chicago.com
Subject: Yes, a toaster


Carrie

You are a girly girl, aren't you? The picture of you wearing your high-heeled boots slipping and sliding across the ice on my lake, tugging your suitcase behind you, plays in my mind.

Yes, a toaster, and it isn't a joke. I want you to have it. I'll call you later tonight. Eleven your time. Work for you?

Finn


From: girlygirl@chicago.com
Sent: November 13, 2013
To: alaskaman@fairbankscable.com
Subject: Waiting for you

Yes, Finn, I'll be here. Call anytime. I'm planning on listening to Christmas music, getting in the mood for the holidays, and sipping hot chocolate. Wish you were here.

Carrie

Finn leaned back in his chair and slowly exhaled. The picture of Carrie sipping hot chocolate and listening to Christmas music while waiting for his call filled his mind. That shouldn't surprise him. Carrie Slayton had dominated his thoughts from the moment she'd left Alaska. And if he was honest, even before that, too.

It wasn't supposed to be like this. He'd assumed that once she was out of sight he'd be able to forget her. That hadn't happened. If anything, it was ten times worse— thoughts of Carrie hounded him. He went to sleep thinking about her, and when he woke, she was right there, filling his mind and his heart.

Even Hennessey missed her. She'd won over his dog in record time, and now that she was gone, Hennessey moped around, his tail between his legs. His eighty-pound dog acted like a lost and lonely puppy. That shouldn't be any surprise, seeing that Finn had reacted much the same since she'd left.

Whatever was happening to him didn't sit well. This was a dead-end relationship, and the sooner he accepted that, the better off they both would be.

And yet . . . Finn couldn't forget Carrie. It was bad enough that she was in the forefront of his thoughts during the day, but it was getting worse, as she had invaded his dreams as well. The kiss they shared was

what had started it all. He'd managed to restrain himself
from taking her in his arms until the very last minute.
Once she was gone, life would right itself again. He even
managed to convince himself this attraction was a simple
matter of proximity. Naturally, they were attracted to
each other, he'd reasoned. They were both young and
single, and they'd been cooped up together for nearly
forty-eight hours. As soon as she was gone, life would
return to normal.

Carrie had been back in Chicago nearly a week now,
and it hadn't happened. It was as if Carrie had indelibly
stamped his heart with her own brand and he was
marked for life.

What Finn feared most was repeating the mistake his
father had made and falling in love with the wrong
woman. After his mother left, Finn's father was never the
same again. When they learned Joan had remarried, it
had about killed the man. In his entire life, his father
had only loved one woman. Now, just like his father,
Finn was irresistibly drawn to a woman who was his
opposite in far too many ways. It was enough to send
warning bells ringing so loud they threatened to activate
an avalanche.

He glanced at his watch, calculating the time
difference between Fairbanks and Chicago. Carrie would

be home by now, unless she was meeting a friend for dinner. Instantly, Finn's gut tightened and his blood pressure spiked. He couldn't bear the thought of Carrie with another man. It drove him to madness. Never having experienced jealousy this strong, he found the emotion distressing and worrisome.

This was the end of it. He was finished walking around like a wounded moose. He made the decision right then and there not to contact her again. But an immediate sense of emptiness and loss settled over him. After talking to her nearly every day and sharing an almost constant flow of emails, cutting off their relationship abruptly wouldn't be good. He'd ease himself out of it, he reasoned, and instantly he felt better. Baby steps. That decided, he made a second decision—no further contact with her for the rest of the day.

Restless now, he stalked the condo and then decided to get out and do something. He headed to a local hangout, had a beer with one of his friends, and before he knew it, he was back in his condo.

Immediately his gaze flew to the telephone. He tilted back his head and stared at the ceiling. Unable to stop himself, he reached for his cell. He wouldn't contact her tomorrow. But for now she was impossible to resist. He dialed Carrie's number, as eager to hear the sound of her voice as a starved man is for nourishment. Oh, yes, he had it bad.

The phone rang, and Carrie nearly stumbled over her own feet in her eagerness to get to it.

"Hello." She nearly blurted out Finn's name but stopped herself in the nick of time. They'd spoken every day, sometimes two and three times. Finn had upgraded his cell phone so they could now text when he was in Fairbanks. He seemed to commute between the cabin and his condo on a regular basis.

"Carrie, it's Mom. What's up with you, honey? We've hardly spoken to you since you got back to Chicago. The only time we've talked is when Dad and I called you about your Christmas gift."

"Oh, Mom," Carrie tried to hide the disappointment in her voice. "I'm sorry. I've been meaning to call." Which was true.

"I have to tell you, honey, Thanksgiving just won't be the same without you."

"I know. I wish I could be there, too." Carrie was upset about it herself. This was the choice she'd made before flying to Alaska. The thought of spending the holiday alone filled her with dismay. She would miss the huge family gathering for the first time in her life.

"It isn't like you not to call."

This was a bit more difficult to explain. "Well, for one thing, being away from my desk for so long means I'm swamped at the office."

"But, honey, you know your father and I are dying to hear what happened in Fairbanks; we've only heard snippets. Tell us more about Finn Dalton. Everyone here wants to know what he's like and if the things he wrote about in his book could really be true."

Carrie's stomach twisted in a huge knot. "Mom, who have you told about me meeting Finn?"

Her mother must have heard the panic in Carrie's voice, because she asked, "Are you keeping it a secret?"

"Yes," she nearly shouted. "This is important. Please don't mention my meeting Finn to anyone, okay?"

"If that's what you want, but surely once the article—"

"There isn't going to be an article."

"But I thought—"

"I know, but I've come to know Finn and want to respect his privacy." Her voice softened as her mind traveled back to the moment when he'd passionately kissed her and held her in his arms before she boarded the flight with Sawyer.

"Carrie?" her mother said. "You better tell me what

happened between you and this wilderness man. And don't try to hide it from me. Clearly there's something going on here; I can hear it in your voice."

Carrie swore her mother had special radar where she was concerned. It seemed she was unable to keep anything from her mother, and perhaps that was a good thing. Besides, Carrie felt like she would burst if she couldn't talk about her feelings for Finn. The way she'd been lately with her head in a cloud was causing all kinds of speculation among her friends, especially Sophie.

"I'm falling in love with Finn Dalton." It felt good to admit it, good to say out loud what was already in her heart.

Her announcement was followed by a short, stunned silence. "After only two days?"

"Does it sound crazy?" Then, before she could stop herself, Carrie blurted out nearly the entire story right to the point when he'd kissed her and asked Carrie not to write the article.

"Love is a strong emotion after such a short acquaintance," her mother warned softly.

"I agree, I do, but I can't help how I feel. It was all sorts of crazy and wonderful. Finn and I were playing cribbage, and I looked up at him and something happened. Something physical. All at once my pulse started racing and I looked at this burly, unshaven man and I thought Finn Dalton was the most attractive, appealing man I'd ever met. At first I tried to ignore it, tried to rationalize this attraction away with an entire list of excuses why a relationship between us simply wouldn't work. It hasn't done me any good. And since I've left Fairbanks, that feeling has grown stronger and stronger. He's on my mind nearly every minute of the day. It's like I'm only half alive since I returned."

"Oh, dear, you do have it bad," her mother said with a sympathetic sigh.

Carrie didn't need her mother to tell her the obvious.

"But surely there's a way for you to write the article and maintain the relationship," her mother suggested. "You could write it and give it to him to read and approve. That way he would have control over what information was released to the public."

"I thought of that, too." Her mind had worked its way around several scenarios, but in the end she feared even approaching Finn with the idea would be a breach of trust.

"Doesn't he realize what that article would do for you and your career?"

"He knows. Finn didn't ask for this notoriety when he wrote his book. He doesn't want the focus to be on him but on the beauty of the land and the adventures that await those willing to explore the great outdoors."

"Well, he should have thought of that before he wrote the book."

In theory, Carrie agreed, but Finn had had no idea how popular his tales of life in Alaska would be. "Do you know why he decided to write *Alone*?" she said, thinking back over a recent conversation. "He said he saw what was happening to men and boys in America, addicted to computer games. People are not getting outside and enjoying the outdoors and the wilderness nearly enough. He wanted to awaken a sense of adventure in people to get excited about what's outside their front doors."

"It worked," her mother said. "I wonder if he knows all the outdoor groups his book has inspired."

"I told him about that, but I don't believe he truly grasps the extent of it. I think he finds it all rather humbling. Finn never sought the national spotlight. In hindsight, I wonder if he'd have written the book if he'd known what a sensation it would cause." His motives were good. If Carrie had learned anything in the time they'd been together, it was that he deeply loved Alaska and that he had respect for nature.

"Sweetheart, just where do you think this relationship

is headed?" her mother asked, clearly concerned for Carrie.

She appreciated her mother's question. "I don't know, and I don't think Finn does, either. For right now, we're taking it one day at a time. And, Mom, you won't believe what he sent me. He actually mailed me a toaster. It looks like an antique."

"A what?"

"You heard me right. A toaster. I realize it probably has some special significance to him that he wanted to share with me. But if that's the case, he hasn't explained it yet. I have it in my kitchen."

Her mother chuckled. "Oh, dear, Carrie. Listen, honey. I don't want to burst your bubble. You're new into this relationship, and this is a honeymoon period, but soon enough reality is going to settle in. I don't want you to set yourself up for heartache. Just be careful, okay?"

"I will, Mom." And while she agreed, Carrie couldn't help thinking that love would see her and Finn through any obstacle. She was crazy for this guy, toaster and all.

Once they'd finished chatting, Carrie returned to her computer. Finn was scheduled to phone, but he hadn't, which concerned her. Just then her cell phone chirped, letting her know she had a text message.

Carrie grabbed her phone.

What are you doing?

Listening to "Mary, Did You Know," which was playing softly in the background. It was one of her favorite Christmas songs.

A little early for Christmas music, isn't it?

Reading Finn's text, she punched in her answer. Not for me. Besides, you have your Christmas decorations in your cabin. How are they holding up?

He responded within seconds. Snowflakes dangling from my ceiling. Utterly ridiculous.

But they are still up?

Yes. Remind me of you.

Very sweet, thank you.

I look at them and think of the stars we saw that night.

That incredible starry night. Makes me miss being with you all the more.

G-r-r-r. Hennessey misses you.

Hennessey? What about you?

Finn texted back a smiley face.

Carrie laughed. She had just tucked her cell phone in her jeans pocket when it rang. A sweet joy went through her when she saw it was Finn. So she was going to get her phone call after all.

"Hi," she said.

"Hi. It seemed ridiculous to be texting you when we could be talking."

"I agree. You must be in Fairbanks. I had no idea you spent that much time in town."

"Generally, I don't. Fact is, until these last few days, it's been weeks since I was at the condo."

In other words, he'd come into town in order to be able to communicate more easily with her. Finn wasn't a romantic man. The fact that he would mail her a toaster told her it was highly unlikely that he would look to win her heart with flowers or jewels.

"I had bread from my toaster for breakfast this morning." She mentioned this so he'd know that she'd put his gift to good use.

"That isn't much of a breakfast."

"I was in a hurry to get to church. I'm in the choir, and we had an early practice for the Christmas pageant."

"You sing, too?"

"I'm an alto. I harmonize well. Come to think of it, I play well with others, too."

"Clearly you're a woman of many talents."

She ran her fingers through a tousle of dark curls. "I'd like to think so."

They spoke for an hour until her cell phone battery was nearly depleted. Before they ended their conversation,

Finn told her he would be out of reach for a couple of days, checking the pipeline outside of Fairbanks.

"I'll survive," she assured him. Although she made it sound as if it wouldn't trouble her, she was already dreading not hearing from him.

"Maybe you'll survive, but I'm not sure about me."

"Finn." She laughed, her heart warmed by his words. "That's the most romantic thing you've ever said to me."

He snickered softly. "I'm not a romantic kind of guy."

"I sort of guessed that, which makes these little comments precious. I'll miss hearing from you, too."

He grumbled as if he didn't quite know how to respond.

"Oh, before you go, I wanted to tell you that I'll be in Chicago for Thanksgiving—it'll be my first alone, but I'll be in Seattle for Christmas." She mentioned this with the hope that he would take the hint and fly down for a visit. Seattle was relatively close to him, much closer than Chicago. When he didn't immediately pick up on her hint, she added, "My parents feel bad that I won't be with everyone on Thanksgiving, so for Christmas they're giving me a ticket to fly home."

"Good idea."

He hesitated and then asked with what seemed like reluctance, "Have you talked to my mother since your return?"

"No. I haven't had a chance to get in touch with her. I know she's anxious to hear what happened with the ring." Truth was, Carrie felt terrible having to tell Joan that her plan had backfired. Given the turn in her relationship with Finn, maybe she'd hang on to the ring a bit longer, rather than returning it at Christmas, as she'd planned.

"Does my mother need anything?" he asked. His voice was low, concerned, and different from the teasing banter they had exchanged earlier.

"She's well physically, if that's what you're asking. As for her other needs, there was only one thing I picked up on."

"And that is?"

Carrie knew she was wading into deep waters, but she felt she had to try. Finn's mother had entrusted her with something precious, and she wanted to repay the favor. "She needs her son."

His response was a dismissive snort.

"That's what I thought you'd say."

"I'll be in touch in a couple of days."

"Okay." Not being able to talk to him for even a short

amount of time would feel like an eternity. "I have a busy week with the holidays close and all."

"You going to be with Harry?" he asked, mentioning the staff photographer.

Now it was Carrie's turn to hesitate. "For a couple of events, and then I'll be out the Tuesday before Thanksgiving with a . . . friend."

"A male friend?"

She didn't want to mislead Finn. "Dave and I set this up a while ago, Finn. Trust me, you don't have anything to worry about."

He grumbled something unintelligible.

This was another romantic jewel he offered her without even realizing what he was doing. Carrie's smile took up her entire face. "I love it that you're jealous."

"I'm not jealous," he insisted. "Just concerned. No guy likes the idea of his girl spending time with some other guy."

Oh, boy, he walked right into that. "Am I your girl, Finn?"

"Would a guy send you a toaster if you weren't?" he asked.

"You have me there," she said, smiling. Her phone beeped, reminding her that her battery was almost dead. "I really need to recharge my phone. Fly safely, Finn."

"I always fly safely."

"And hug Hennessey for me."

"What about me?"

"Do you want a hug, too?"

"I'll take that as a bare minimum, but I'd like a whole lot more."

"So would I," she whispered, before she ended the call.

# Chapter 9

"What's with you lately?" Sophie asked Wednesday afternoon as they waited in line to order lunch.

"What do you mean?" Carrie pretended to be reading the menu posted on the wall above the cashier. She almost always ordered the same thing. Egg-salad sandwich on wheat with a small garden salad, ranch dressing on the side.

"Ever since you were away you've been . . . I don't know, different, I guess. Happier."

Carrie smiled. Oh, yes, she was happier.

"You've met someone, haven't you?"

How could she deny it and keep a straight face? "Could be."

"Carrie, it isn't like you to keep secrets. It's the guy who sent you that joke gift, isn't it?"

"The toaster isn't a joke, but yes, and if you must know, his name is Paul." *Middle name,* she added silently.

"Paul is from Seattle?"

Technically, that was where Finn was born. "Yes."

"What's his story? Is he married? Is that the reason you're keeping this to yourself?"

"Married? Of course not." It irritated Carrie that Sophie would believe she'd even consider dating a married man. "You know, I'm thinking I'll order the curried chicken-salad sandwich instead of my usual egg salad. I'm in the mood to live on the edge."

"You're changing the subject."

"Yes. Get the hint, Sophie. I'll tell you more when there's more to tell. For now, I'm not talking."

"Fine, then, have it your way," Sophie pouted.

Carrie's cell phone beeped.

I'm back. It was Finn.

"It's him, isn't it?" Sophie demanded, attempting to look over Carrie's shoulder.

Carrie ignored her and stepped up to the counter to place her lunch order. When it was Sophie's turn, she grabbed her phone and texted back. Can't talk now.

Have you missed me?

Oh, yes. Am having lunch with snoopy friend.

Got ya. In an hour?

OK.

She dropped her phone back inside her purse just before Sophie rejoined her. They found a vacant spot, set their order numbers on the table, and then went for their drinks. Carrie was antsy to talk to Finn. Two days had never seemed so long. She was dying to know if he'd missed talking to her nearly half as much as she'd missed chatting with him.

Carrie had her coffee and Sophie her soft drink when they reclaimed their table.

"We should talk about the party," Sophie said. Their orders arrived, and she thanked the waiter with a smile.

Party? What party? Then Carrie remembered that just before she left for Alaska they'd decided to host a small party in Carrie's condo after Thanksgiving. Her place was bigger and could accommodate more guests.

"I was thinking the first week of December. Friday or Saturday."

"Sounds good." Carrie mentally reviewed her calendar. As far as she could remember, both days were clear.

"If we don't get the word out soon, it won't happen. Besides, everyone gets so busy this time of year."

Sophie was a party girl, and Carrie had agreed, looking to make the most of the holiday season.

"I thought we'd throw together a few appetizers and bring out the eggnog. Four or five couples should keep it manageable. We don't need to make a huge thing out of it—just a few friends getting together to celebrate the holidays."

"Ah, sure."

Sophie reached for the pepper shaker and doused her Oriental chicken salad. "You going to ask Dave?"

He was Carrie's Tuesday-night theater date. "Probably not."

"Because of this other guy?"

Sophie was digging for information, but Carrie wasn't going to let anything out. In response, she shrugged.

"David's a prize, you know."

"For someone else, maybe."

"From what I've seen, he'd like to be more than a friend."

Carrie had sensed as much. But even before she met Finn she knew it wasn't happening for her. She felt vastly different when it came to Finn. He was a man's man. Dave was personable and fun, but he wouldn't be able to last a day on his own in an Alaskan winter. He wouldn't even know where to start in order to survive. Oh, he could dress like a male model and flatter a woman with compliments and sweet talk. In simple terms, he wasn't, and would never be, another Finn.

As they munched through their meal they quickly pared down the guest list. Sophie promised to send out email invites that afternoon. A little more than two weeks wasn't much notice, but it should be adequate.

Eager to hear from Finn, Carrie rushed back to the office and straight to her cubicle. She still had one sleeve in her coat when she grabbed her cell phone and texted Finn.

I'm back in the office.

It didn't take long for him to reply. Snoopy friend?

Need to be careful; suspicions running rampant. Told her you were from Seattle, which you are, right?

Born there.

Close enough.

Sophie?

Yes. Talk tonight?

OK.

Carrie had her phone tucked back inside her purse and her coat off when her desk phone rang. She answered the way she always did. "Carrie Slayton."

"Carrie?"

The voice on the other end of the line was vaguely familiar.

"It's Joan Reese, Finn Dalton's mother. I hope you don't mind me contacting you, but I hadn't heard from you and I've been anxious for news of my son."

Carrie felt dreadful that she'd delayed getting in touch with Finn's mother. "Joan, I am so sorry. I've been meaning to call." She started to make a convenient excuse, the way she had with her own family, then stopped herself.

"Were you able to talk to Finn?" Joan asked.

"Yes." Carrie couldn't find the words to tell this gentle woman that Finn wanted nothing to do with her or the wedding band Joan had asked her to deliver.

"Did you give him the ring?"

"I tried." That should tell her what had happened without Carrie going into a long explanation.

"Oh." In a single word, her disappointment rang like a cathedral bell.

Carrie lowered her voice for fear someone might be listening in on the conversation. "I spent two days alone with him at his cabin outside of Fairbanks. Well, his dog was with us, too."

"How is he?" Joan asked, with such longing that it nearly brought tears to Carrie's eyes.

Carrie hardly knew how to answer, knowing she meant more than Finn's physical well-being. Joan hungered for information, and Carrie didn't have those kinds of answers. "He's doing well," she started off. "He looks good. He has a big dog named Hennessey."

"Hennessey?"

"Yes. When I first saw him I thought he was a wolf, interested in dinner and that meal was me." She hoped the story would bring levity to their conversation.

Joan laughed softly. "Paul must have named him. Hennessey was his mother's maiden name."

Carrie remembered how the large dog had spent the night warming her and longed to see him again.

Joan hesitated. "Finn wouldn't take the ring, would he?"

"No, but he did ask after you."

"He did?" How quickly joy flooded her words. "That gives me hope."

"It's a positive sign. Given time, I think Finn will come around, I really do." Carrie couldn't leave the older woman without some positive news. Perhaps in time Carrie would be able to influence Finn to give his mother another chance.

Joan softly sighed. "I hope you're right. I really appreciate your efforts."

"He might not realize it yet, but one day Finn will figure out that he needs you, too."

"Thank you, Carrie." Joan said, and she seemed to struggle to sound encouraged. "I won't keep you any longer. I apologize for contacting you at your work."

"Joan, before I let you go I need to ask you something . . ."

"Of course, anything."

"Finn mailed me a gift. It's a toaster, a really old one. I asked him about it, but his answers have been vague. Is there some significance to it?"

His mother started to laugh. "He gave you the toaster?"

"Yes. I have it in my kitchen . . . I've been using it."

Joan exhaled and seemed to be gathering her thoughts. "Paul bought that toaster for me when we were first dating. My goodness, I had no idea he'd kept it. That toaster is nearly forty years old. It was the first sign I had that Paul had any feelings for me."

"Why do you think Finn would want me to have it?"

"My dear, isn't it obvious?" she asked, and appeared to get real enjoyment out of the telling. "My son is crazy about you. He's repeating what his father did when he first fell in love with me. Finn is telling you the only way he knows how that you're important to him."

"He's important to me, too."

The line went silent for a moment. "Oh, dear. Are you in love with my son?"

"I think so," Carrie said, lowering her voice. She wasn't sure why she hesitated. "Yes," she said, plainly, distinctly. They'd known each other less than a month and yet her heart knew. No man had ever made her feel the way she did about Finn.

"Proceed carefully, my dear," Joan warned. "If Finn is anything like his father, and I suspect he is, then he doesn't give his heart lightly; he loves deeply, completely, and when he's hurt he'll react like a wounded grizzly bear."

Carrie mulled over Finn's mother's words the rest of the afternoon. The conversation with her own mother lingered in her mind as well. She and Finn were very different people, living in entirely different worlds. She was a girly girl, just as her email address claimed, and he lived and worked in the Alaskan wilderness. The practical side of Carrie reminded her that they had little in common, but her heart was unwilling to listen.

Carrie's mother had referred to this as the honeymoon part of the relationship, when they were so caught up in the intensity of their feelings that they willingly ignored their differences. It was easy to do, which was exactly what her mother was trying to tell her.

Finn's mother, too, had issued her own dire warning. It seemed everyone she told about her and Finn was filled with doubts about the two of them. One reason Carrie hadn't told Sophie about Finn was because she knew her best friend would become a naysayer as well, and Carrie didn't want to hear it.

That evening Carrie was anxious to talk to Finn. She sat on the sofa with her legs tucked under her and the phone clenched tightly in her hand, ready to answer the instant he rang. Her thick, wild hair was tied at the base of her neck with a scrunchie.

By the time he phoned, Carrie felt ready to weep. "I'm so glad you called," she blurted out the minute she heard his voice.

"What's wrong?" He was immediately concerned.

"Your mother. My mother."

"What's going on? You talked to my mother?" He didn't sound happy about it, either.

"Oh, sure, get upset with me, too, that's all I need."

"Carrie, take a deep breath and start at the beginning."

She inhaled deeply and then exhaled. "My mom and I spoke recently, and she warned me about falling for you . . . she said right now nothing seems impossible, but eventually we're going to have to face our differences."

The line went silent as he seemed to take in her mother's words of wisdom. "And my mother said the same thing," he said gruffly, sounding annoyed.

"More or less."

"And that worries you?"

"Yes. I don't want it to, but it does. It's been nearly three weeks since I last saw you and it feels like an eternity. Is it really possible to feel this strongly about someone I've known only a short while?"

"Do you want to call it quits now and save us both a lot of hassle and heartache?" he asked starkly.

"No." Her response was vehement and instant. "Are you saying that's what you want?"

"No way. I found myself whistling the other day. I haven't whistled since I was a kid. I climbed into bed at the cabin the other night and I felt your presence from just that small amount of time you slept in my bed. I rested better than I have in years."

"Oh, Finn, you make me want to cry." Carrie didn't know why she'd thought this man couldn't be romantic.

"Sawyer just looks at me and shakes his head, as if he no longer recognizes me. I'm not alone, either. Hennessey mopes around the cabin, looking lost and miserable."

"It's the same with me. What's happened to us? I think about you and then my insides get all mushy and I feel like I want to cry because I have no idea when I'll see you again," she whispered.

She heard the sound of him exhaling. "We don't have to make any decisions tonight, do we?"

"No," she agreed.

"I can't give you up yet, Carrie."

"Do you have to give me up at all?" she asked. "Do I have to give you up?"

"Not now, and hopefully not for a very long time."

"Good," she whispered, "because I don't think I could bear it."

"Great," he said with some enthusiasm. "Now that we have that settled, let's talk about something else. Tell me about this hot date of yours."

"Oh, Finn, honestly, you have nothing to fear from Dave."

"Ah, so his name is Dave."

"He's a nice guy, but he would never think to give a woman a toaster. He doesn't have a heart nearly as big as yours."

"You realize I'm going to be worrying about you with this guy the entire time you're out with him."

His words cheered her considerably. "I'm glad to hear it."

"You are?"

"Well, sure. It will keep you on your toes. If this kind of competition continues, I could end up with a can opener that matches that toaster."

# *Chapter 10*

The night of her dinner date with Dave, Carrie hurried home from the office in order to change clothes. Cool, suave, sophisticated Dave. Finn had been suspiciously quiet all day. She hadn't received a single text from him in nearly twenty-four hours, which was unusual. She knew he was concerned about her going to the theater, even with a friend, and seemed to view any man she saw as a potential threat. It was clear he didn't have a clue how head-over-heels nuts she was over him.

Perhaps she was living in a fool's garden, not thinking about the future. Frankly, she didn't care what chances anyone gave their relationship. Finn felt as much a part of her now as her arms and legs.

She changed clothes but kept her cell phone handy, hoping to hear the ding that would tell her she had a text message. The earlier one she'd sent him remained unanswered. Perhaps he'd returned to the lake cabin, but it seemed he would have mentioned it, if that was the case.

Once she refreshed her makeup, she glanced out the window and saw that the snow, which had been threatening most of the afternoon, had started to fall in thick flakes. With the holidays so close, everyone seemed preoccupied. Carrie had gotten three invitations to parties and other social events from friends. Sophie had invited Carrie to join her family for Thanksgiving. Knowing she would be alone, even Harry had extended an invite. Carrie had declined both invitations, feeling she would be an add-on. She would have her own Thanksgiving, she decided, and make the best of it by herself.

The last time she'd seen snow she'd been with Finn and Hennessey. The reminder made her miss them both dreadfully.

Unable to bear this silence any longer, she reached for her cell and typed out with practiced ease. Miss you.

Almost right away she got a response. Good.

Where have you been all day? Finn had to know she'd been anxiously waiting to hear from him.

In the air. Still have your hot date tonight?

In the air? That didn't make sense—a flight to Fairbanks from his cabin was less than thirty minutes. Are you jealous?

You bet.

Carrie grinned, and a warm sensation came over her. It's snowing here; makes me miss you all the more.

I know it's snowing in Chicago.

You know it's snowing?????

Big, fat flakes.

Carrie gasped, and her fingers moved with urgency across the tiny alphabet on her cell phone. Finn, where are you?

Chicago.

She hardly had time to take in the fact that Finn was in town before her phone rang. She hit the answer button so hard the cell nearly dropped out of her hands.

"Surprise," he whispered.

Carrie wanted to laugh and cry at the same time. Laugh because she was so happy and excited and then weep because she had this stupid date and wouldn't be able to see him until the end of the evening.

"Where are you?"

He named a local hotel about two blocks from her

condo. "I know it's crazy, my being here. I didn't want you to be alone over Thanksgiving."

"I don't care if it's crazy or not; I'm too happy to care." Carrie just hoped she didn't embarrass herself when she first saw him by launching into his arms and bursting into tears. She'd dreamed about seeing him again. He hadn't said a word that he was planning this. Not a single solitary word.

"Do you still have to go to the theater?" he asked, and then instantly withdrew the question. "Forget I asked. Of course you do. I'll be here at the hotel waiting, and when you get back to your apartment, let me know."

Her doorbell chimed, announcing Dave's arrival. "I hope you realize this is torture," she told Finn on her way to answer the front door.

"For you or for me?"

"For us both." Carrie had no idea how she was going to get through this evening, knowing Finn was in town.

"Go. It'll be fine," Finn encouraged her.

"Okay, but you're going to suffer for doing this to me."

He chuckled and ended the call.

Carrie took a moment to compose herself before she opened the door. Dave was impeccably dressed for the evening. He really was an attractive man, but she didn't feel even the slightest stirrings for him. Just thinking about Finn waiting for her in his hotel room had her pulse spinning at the rate of a jet engine.

The Christmas musical they went to see, which had gotten rave reviews, didn't hold Carrie's attention, but to be fair, she doubted she would have appreciated anything outside of a five-alarm fire. Somehow she got through the evening, although she felt it was only fair to tell Dave that she'd met someone else. Their relationship had never really gone beyond friendship, and he took her news well.

Straight from the theater, Dave drove her to her home and briefly parked outside the condo complex. The snow had stopped, but traffic was a mess. It went without saying that he didn't need to see her up. She thanked him for the evening, and then before she climbed out of the car she impulsively hugged him. He'd been decent and thoughtful, and she was grateful for his friendship.

"I hope it works with you and the other guy," he said, and didn't seem to have any hard feelings.

"I do, too." Carrie wished that more than anything.

"He's a lucky guy."

"I'll let him know you said so." She smiled as she said it.

Climbing out of the car, she gathered her coat more

securely around her and made a dash for the building's entrance. Dave waited until she was inside the foyer, and Carrie waved before he drove off. The instant he was out of sight, she opened her clutch to retrieve her cell phone. Right away, she sent Finn a text.

I'm home.

I know.

She glanced up to find Finn standing on the other side of the building's glass door. For a moment, all she could do was stare at him. She shivered with the cold, but he wore no jacket. All he had on was a yellow-and-black plaid shirt, jeans, and boots. In her entire life she'd never seen a more strongly appealing man. Hurrying to the locked security door, she opened it for him. Even before he was inside, she was wrapped in his embrace.

Carrie looped her arms around his neck, hugging him and laughing with joy. Right away, Finn swept her off her feet. With his arms around her waist, he lifted her so that her shoes dangled several inches off the ground. With her hands framing his bearded face, they kissed as if they couldn't get enough, as if they meant to consume each other right in the center of the lobby.

A man's voice broke through the fog of longing and joy. "Ms. Slayton? Ms. Slayton?"

Reluctantly, Carrie ended the kiss and looked over

her shoulder to find Lester, the security guard, closely studying her.

"You know this man?" Lester asked.

She smiled and nodded. "Lester, this is—"

Finn released her and stretched out his hand to the guard. "Paul. Paul Dalton."

"Glad to meet you, Paul. I apologize if I was rude earlier."

"Not a problem."

Carrie was curious to know what that was all about. "Let's go upstairs," she said, and steered Finn toward the elevator. She waited until they were inside and the doors had closed. "I'm glad you were clearheaded enough to tell him your name is Paul."

Finn smiled down at her "Clearheaded? You're joking, right?"

Carrie laughed and cuddled close to his side. They had their arms around each other. "What's this about Lester being rude?"

"It's nothing. He didn't like the idea of unsavory types hanging around the building and asked what my business was."

"Unsavory types?"

"Shhh, just let me kiss you again."

Carrie wasn't about to argue with him. They were

completely consumed with each other when the elevator stopped on the twenty-fifth floor and the door glided open. Finn reluctantly broke off the kiss and thrust out his arm to stop the doors from closing on them.

Using her code, Carrie let them into her apartment, wondering what Finn would think when he stepped inside the ultra-exclusive high-rise. It was a one-bedroom unit that she'd rented because of its close proximity to the newspaper office and the incredible views of the city it offered.

Staring out the picture window, Finn stood with his back to her. "I'm a bit out of my element."

Wrapping her arms around him, she pressed the side of her face against his back. "I think we're both way out of our comfort zones."

He chuckled and folded his rough, muscled hands over hers. "True enough."

"I'm so glad you're here."

"It was either fly to see you or go slowly mad wondering about you and that pretty boy."

"You saw Dave?"

"I saw you hug him. He's darn lucky he didn't try to kiss you; otherwise, I would have been forced to drag him out of that car and send him flying into the closest snowbank."

Carrie laughed at the mental picture. Dave was a pretty boy, but he wouldn't have stood still for Finn's he-man tactics.

"You think I'm joking?"

"Oh, Finn, if only you knew how close you are to my heart."

He turned and nearly crushed her in his arms before he slowly released her. "I've never been the jealous sort, but Carrie, you . . . . you make me feel things." Frowning, he rubbed his chest. "One kiss just before Sawyer took you away and you unbalanced my entire life. I hardly know myself any longer."

"Do you like having your life unbalanced?" she asked, noting how dark his face grew with the confession.

"I don't know. It's never happened quite like this."

She kissed him, letting her lips linger over his. When she pulled away, he groaned softly. "Perhaps I could grow used to it," he whispered.

"I'm thinking I could as well," she confessed.

After a while she brewed them each a cup of coffee, and then they sat and talked away half the night. They bounced from one subject to the next as if it'd been months since they'd last spoken. It felt as if they'd known each other their entire lives. Finn talked about the second book he'd written. It was finished, but he wasn't sure it was as good as the first one.

"That's a problem when a first book is such a success," she said thoughtfully.

"How do you mean?"

"Well, there's all this pressure for you to repeat the performance of the first book. That alone is intimidating enough."

Finn agreed. "New York keeps asking me when they can see this second manuscript, and I've been putting them off, although it's been finished for quite some time."

"Would you like me to read it?" she asked.

"Would you?"

"Of course." It was an honor that he trusted her enough to give her this opportunity.

"You'll be honest with me?"

"If that's what you want."

"I do."

With anyone else she would have doubted their sincerity, but not with Finn.

It must have been close to three in the morning before Finn announced it was time for him to go back to his hotel. Carrie resisted the urge to ask him to stay. They both knew that it wouldn't take much encouragement on either of their parts to convince him to spend the night. She had to go to work in the morning but would be off early. Most of the staff would be away from their desks for the Thanksgiving holiday.

Reluctantly, Carrie walked him to the door.

"Can I see you tomorrow?" he asked, his arms around her.

"Please."

"Any more social obligations I need to know about?"

"Nope. The entire holiday is free . . . well, other than church. The choir is singing. You'll come, won't you?"

He frowned and then nodded.

Carrie rewarded him with a lengthy kiss. "Church might actually do you some good, and then next week is the party."

He frowned again. "What party?"

"The Christmas one Sophie and I are throwing right here. You must come, you really must."

He certainly didn't look keen to join in the festivities. "The first week of December? You'll be here, won't you?"

"Ah . . ."

"See if you can change your flight, Finn. I need to prove to everyone that you're real. If you think you're the only one who's not himself, then you're wrong. My friends claim they hardly know me anymore."

"Carrie, I'll never fit in with your life here."

She didn't argue. Instead, she pressed her hand to the side of his jaw, her eyes round and pleading.

Finn snickered softly, and Carrie knew she'd won.

"Could I refuse you anything?" he asked.

"Good to know." She hugged him, fearing if they kissed again they wouldn't be able to stop.

He grumbled but didn't argue.

"I promise the rewards will be worth any discomfort."

"Rewards?" His dark eyes brightened.

"Yes. We can talk about those later."

He left her then, and while she was practically asleep on her feet, Carrie was far too happy and excited to let go of the exquisite sensation of knowing Finn was only a couple of blocks away, and would be with her for several days.

# Chapter 11

Late Wednesday morning Finn unloaded the last of the groceries into Carrie's refrigerator. Shopping for their Thanksgiving dinner had been an experience he never wanted to repeat. While she was at the office he decided to make good use of his time and get what they needed for their meal. If ever he wanted a lesson in the differences between their lives, this was it. The trip to the grocery store had taken him hours.

Finn knew his way around a kitchen, his father had made sure of that. But the meat he was most familiar with didn't come from a food market. He found the selection of vegetables and fresh fruit mind-boggling. He had to admit he was impressed. It was like walking into the Garden of Eden. In Alaska, especially at this time of year, fresh fruits and vegetables were at a premium. They were available in limited quantities, but the prices were astronomical.

He glanced at his watch. Carrie should arrive home anytime now. Just thinking about her produced a sense of lightness that he'd rarely experienced. His decision to fly to Chicago had been last-minute. If he'd been smart he would have planned this trip much earlier.

After all Carrie had gone through in order to find him, he was determined she not be alone over Thanksgiving. She was close to her family, which was something Finn had never experienced. His father had been his only relative, though Carrie would be quick to remind him that his mother was living. But she'd been out of his life since he was a kid and he had nothing to say to her. He loved hearing Carrie talk about her family and their traditions. It made him feel good to know how deeply she valued these relationships; it was something he envied. The more he got to know Carrie, the more he cared about her. He tried to ignore the feeling that he was starting to care more for her than he should. More than was wise for either of them.

Finn pushed those thoughts aside for now. He was

determined to make this a Thanksgiving they would both remember.

The door opened and Carrie breezed in, breathless and excited. "Finn?" she called out.

"In here." He had the turkey in the sink and the countertops lined with a variety of food.

She rounded the corner and came to an abrupt halt, her beautiful blue eyes widening. "What in heaven's name is this?" Not waiting for his answer, she launched herself into his arms and buried her face in his neck.

Finn wrapped his arms around her and breathed in the fresh scent of her. In all his life, nothing had felt more right than having Carrie in his arms. If he was living in a dream world, then he never wanted to wake up. She smelled of roses and sunshine. Clinging to him, she swallowed tightly but didn't say a word.

"It's our Thanksgiving dinner," he explained, probably unnecessarily. "I plan to cook for you."

Her arms remained tightly clenched around his neck. "Thank you. Oh, thank you," she whispered.

What struck him was the fact that Carrie thanked him when he was the one who should be grateful. For an instant his throat clogged and he found it impossible to speak. He held her close and then they were kissing, so hungry for each other that breathing no longer seemed necessary. The taste, the feel, the need he had for this one woman was all the oxygen he would ever require. In a single moment all the hassles of traveling from Alaska, the crowded grocery store, and every other irritation he'd experienced evaporated. Being with Carrie was worth all of it.

Finn realized this emotional high, this linking of their hearts, was temporary. He'd long ago accepted that their time together was destined to be limited. He tried not to think about it. One day they would both need to face reality, but it wouldn't be this day. He hoped whatever it was they shared would last, and in the same breath he felt he had to accept that it probably wouldn't. People change, and what had seemed right could suddenly go very wrong. One day Carrie was sure to wake up to their differences. Thus far they'd managed to look past the fact that they were polar opposites. As soon as she stopped, and long before he was ready to deal with letting her go, she would end their relationship. Finn had seen it often enough. His own mother had walked out on him and his father. They were a good example of what happened when a man and a woman who didn't belong together ignored what should have been clear from the beginning.

Gradually and with a great deal of reluctance, Finn released her. Carrie tried to hide the tears that shimmered in her eyes. Because he knew they embarrassed her, he pretended not to notice. One thing that did catch his attention, though, was the reddish marks his beard had caused on the tender skin of her face. He rubbed his hand down the sides of his jaw and felt his prickly whiskers. His thick beard offered his face protection against the bitter cold, but for Carrie he would do away with it. Fact was, he hardly remembered what he looked like without it.

"I was thinking this was going to be the worst Thanksgiving of my life," Carrie confessed.

"Not on my watch," Finn countered, and, taking her hand, he raised it to his lips and kissed the inside of her palm.

Their Thanksgiving meal was everything Finn had hoped it would be. The turkey was cooked to perfection and the stuffing was delicious. In fact, the entire meal was the best he could remember outside of his early child-hood. His mother's cornbread stuffing had been his fa-vorite, and he'd taken delight in wolfing it down in large quantities. Along with that long-buried memory came others, reminding him that at one point, his parents had been happy together. And then they weren't. He knew the lessons from their marriage and divorce remained deeply engraved in his psyche, but he hadn't minded that until now. Finn shook his head, needing to dispel the image of his parents and those early Thanksgivings. He wanted to focus on the present, here with Carrie.

The table was covered with partially empty serving dishes, and their plates were practically clean when Carrie leaned back in her chair and groaned. "If I swallow another bite I will explode. Oh, Finn, you're a wonderful chef."

Finn basked in her praise although the meal had been a team effort. She'd done a good deal of the preparation work.

They sat across from each other. "What were your Thanksgivings like as a child?" she asked.

"Funny you should ask. I was just thinking about that myself." The memories wrapped themselves around him, warming him. "Mom got up at the crack of dawn and got the turkey in the oven so I woke to the smell of it roasting. I don't think I'll ever forget that. She'd be busy baking and cooking, and Dad would offer to help."

"He would? I don't picture your dad as someone who would volunteer to help cook."

"He wasn't. To the best of my memory, he only offered at Thanksgiving. I think he was more of a nuisance than anything. I suspect what he wanted was to be close to Mom. Dad's main job was to peel the potatoes."

"What was your job?"

"To eat the potatoes," Finn teased.

Just the way he knew she would, Carrie laughed. "Then, after dinner, Mom would bring out this Nativity set and she'd let me set it up on the fireplace mantel. I still have it."

"Do you put it out for Christmas?" she asked.

If anyone else had asked, he'd deny it, but with Carrie he couldn't. Everything was different with Carrie.

"What about Thanksgiving after your mother left?" she asked.

He shrugged. "It was just Dad and me, and maybe a few of my father's single friends."

"Did you ever leave Alaska?"

"Why would we?"

"Vacations?"

"Alaska has everything I would ever want, but on occasion I did travel. I went to France once, and England. A couple of times I had business meetings in Texas and got a kick out of the lone-star attitude, thinking they're so big. Minnesota brags about its ten thousand lakes. Do you know how many lakes are in Alaska?"

"I don't have a clue."

"Over a million."

"A million!"

Finn knew she was impressed just by the way she said it.

"You were born in Seattle. Do you have any memories of life there?" she asked.

"None. Mom and Dad moved to Fairbanks when I was a baby. They bought a house there and Dad kept it, but he built a cabin on the tundra as well."

"And then you did, too."

"My father built that house with his own two hands, and he taught me everything he knew. I was fortunate to learn I could survive on my own in the wilderness if it was ever necessary. Some of those experiences are included in *Alone*, but I have a lot more stories to tell."

Carrie leaned forward and pushed her plate aside. "I don't see why you refuse to give interviews. It's not like you're truly a recluse, and from what I've seen you would even be good on television."

He sighed and leaned back while he formulated his answer. When the book had first started selling, his publisher had wanted him to do interviews. But Finn hadn't signed up to have his personal life invaded. He wanted nothing to do with that side of the business. From that point forward, his publisher automatically rejected all interviews and invitations for appearances. All the interest and attention embarrassed him. It wasn't until reporters started making trips to Fairbanks that he grew irritated and stubborn.

"The simple answer is that I like my privacy."

She mulled that over, and he half expected her to bring up the article she wanted to write. She didn't, and gradually the tension between his shoulder blades eased. Maybe he could trust her. He certainly wanted to.

Their conversation drifted to other subjects, and Finn was grateful. He didn't often talk about his childhood. Carrie's had been wrapped around happy memories of cousins and family gatherings. Finn hadn't experienced that and didn't realize all he'd missed. He enjoyed listening to her stories. If he ever had a family, this was what he would wish for his own children.

They cleaned the kitchen together, music playing in the background, using any time they were in close proximity to kiss. Hands down, this had been the best Thanksgiving of his life.

Once they finished with the cleanup, Finn brought out the cribbage board.

"What are we playing for?" she asked, as she sat down and reached for the deck.

He shrugged. "Whatever you wish."

Carrie's smile widened. "Oh, how tempting. Okay, if I win, we go shopping in the morning."

"Shopping?" He couldn't believe she would even suggest something so out of his comfort zone. He knew from previous conversations this was something Carrie and her mother did every Black Friday. "This is a joke, right?"

"No joke. I want you to meet my friends, and right now they'll take one look and know you're from Alaska. From there, it'll be easy to make the leap that you're Finn Dalton."

Gauging by the determination in her eyes, Finn realized it didn't matter what cards he was dealt. Within a matter of hours he would be on the Chicago streets, credit card in hand, and he'd do it gladly because Carrie had asked him to.

The deep-dish sausage and pepperoni pizza sat in the middle of the table in front of Carrie and Finn. Try as she might, she couldn't take her eyes off him. He was gorgeous. His beard was gone, and his hair neatly trimmed. His jaw was clearly defined, and his lips were full and enticing.

"Stop looking at me," he said, clearly uncomfortable with her scrutiny.

"Sorry, I can't help myself. You look more scrumptious than that pizza." The woodsman had disappeared, and in his place sat Prince Charming. Finn was handsome—well, in her eyes, anyway—and if the glances she saw coming from other women in the restaurant were anything to go by, she wasn't alone in thinking so. The transformation was total. Finn exuded vigor and strength, and she found it nearly impossible to keep from staring.

"You have to admit this is the best pizza you've ever tasted," she said, in an effort to keep the conversation going. If she was drooling, it wasn't over the food.

"All right, you win. Chicago pizza isn't half bad, but you have to promise to try reindeer-sausage pizza the next time you're in Alaska."

"I wouldn't miss it," she teased.

"I'm serious."

She loved the idea that he assumed she would visit Alaska again, and frankly, she wasn't opposed to the idea, especially if it meant she would be with Finn. It didn't hurt that he loved pizza as much as she did, either.

"You know what's funny?" he said, wiping the grease from his fingers with a paper napkin. "I keep fighting the urge to text you."

Carrie laughed because she'd experienced the same feeling. It was the usual way they communicated and had become such a habit that it felt odd not to be exchanging texts even when they sat across the table from each other.

"We're done shopping, right?"

"We are unless you have a secret desire to face the maddening crowds yet again."

He scoffed. "Hardly. I've seen about as many people in one day as I can handle. I'm starting to feel claustrophobic. Is it always like this in the city?"

"Always. Sometimes worse, although not often. Black Friday is a special, magical day." Carrie hid a smile. One disgruntled look from Finn told her he could do without the holiday craziness. "But you haven't been to Navy Pier yet."

"Another time," he pleaded. "I don't think I can take much more of these crowds, let alone the noise."

"Okay." Carrie had no complaints, watching as he once again ran his hand over his smooth cheeks as though he felt naked.

He'd arrived at her apartment that morning clean shaven, and for just an instant she hadn't recognized the man standing in front of her. She hadn't asked him to shave and had been both shocked and delighted.

"And you keep staring at me."

"Sorry, I can't stop myself. I had no idea you were such a hunk."

He chuckled as if she'd made a joke, but she wasn't kidding. The minute her friends took one look at him, they'd be all over Finn, especially Sophie. She frowned, disliking the thought.

"What's wrong?" he asked, as he paid their tab and collected their purchases. Finn reached for her hand, gripping it in his own as they started out of the restaurant.

It amazed her how easily he read her mood. "What makes you think anything is wrong?"

"You're frowning."

"I just got an inkling of how you felt with me spending the evening with Dave." They wove their way around busy tables toward the front of the well-known Chicago pizza restaurant.

He paused, frowning, his brow folding into thick ripples. "I doubt that."

"I was imagining my friends meeting you, and I realized they are going to want you for themselves. You're mine, Finn, all mine."

His eyes grew dark and serious. His grip tightened on her hand. "No one is going to turn my head, Carrie. It simply isn't possible."

Carrie and Finn walked back to her condo, bundles in hand. Until that morning Finn mentioned that the only clothes shopping he'd done in years had been through catalogs or online. It'd been a true test of the strength of their relationship when it came to choosing dress slacks and a sweater for him. All in all, he'd been more than patient, but she could appreciate his unease.

Once back at her condo, Finn collapsed onto her sofa, spreading out his arms along the back cushion. Her tree was up but had yet to be decorated, and although it was only four feet tall, it took up one entire corner of her living room. Finn had placed a gift under it first thing that morning. She eyed it now, wrapped in plain brown paper.

"Curious?" he asked.

"Very." She picked it up, held it close to her ear, and shook it.

"Any guesses?"

"I doubt it's a can opener."

He grinned. "You're way off base."

"Do you want to tell me?"

"And ruin the surprise? No way. You have to wait until Christmas."

Carrie reluctantly set it back down. "You're taunting me, and that simply isn't fair."

"I think you'll be pleased" was all Finn was willing to tell her. Over the years she'd received a variety of gifts from the men she'd dated, but Finn's gifts were distinctive in every way. It wasn't likely she would ever forget that toaster.

Carrie went over to her television and removed a DVD from her collection.

"We're watching a movie?" Finn asked.

"Yes. It's tradition."

"What movie?"

"You'll see in a minute."

"Is it a romance? I don't think I could sit through a chick flick—not after the last three hours."

"Shush." She sat down close to him and reached for her remote control, pushing the appropriate button.

Right away he slid his arm around her shoulders and then let it drop. "*The Bishop's Wife*?" he muttered as the title flashed across the screen. "It's in black and white."

"Have you seen it?"

"Yes, years ago . . ."

"It's my favorite Christmas movie."

"Ah . . ."

"Shhh, you'll miss the introduction."

His arm was back, and she pressed her head against his shoulder. "Just relax and enjoy."

He grumbled, but she noticed that he was soon into the movie. Every now and again he would lean forward and kiss her temple. Carrie snuggled into his embrace. She loved that they could cuddle and be this close.

"Listen up. This is one of the best lines of any movie ever." Carrie mouthed the words along with Cary Grant as he spoke to Loretta Young.

Finn sat up slightly. "You've memorized the movie?"

"Parts of it. Like I said, it's one of my favorites." It thrilled her that he was with her and they could view it together. What she loved was how much he seemed to be enjoying it, too.

"Just how many times have you watched this silly movie?"

"It isn't a silly movie," she insisted, knowing that he enjoyed teasing her.

"Have you ever seen *The Replacement Killers*?"

"Yuck, no."

"Yuck? It's a great movie."

"Tell you what," Carrie whispered, tilting her head back and kissing the underside of his clean-shaven jaw. "I'll watch it with you one day, as long as you promise to hold me just like this."

He smiled down on her. "Deal."

The phone rang shortly after the movie ended. It was

Sophie. "A group of us are going to Logan's for drinks. Can you meet us?"

"Let me check."

"Check?" Sophie repeated.

"I have company. F— Paul is in town."

"Seattle Paul? The guy who's got you walking around with your head in the clouds Paul?"

"One and the same." Finn eyed her closely. Carrie was sure he was able to hear both sides of the conversation.

"You didn't say anything about him coming to Chicago."

"I didn't know. It was a surprise."

"Well, bring him. I, for one, am dying to meet this guy."

"Hold on." Carrie pressed her cell against her chest. "What do you think? Do you want to go out tonight?"

"Do you?"

She shrugged. "I'd like you to meet my friends."

He hesitated and then nodded. "Okay."

She leaned forward and kissed him soundly on the lips.

"I could grow accustomed to these little rewards you so willingly hand out," he murmured as he gripped her hand.

Carrie smiled and brought the cell back to her ear. "What time?"

"Does eight work for you?"

"Perfect. See you then."

Sophie hesitated. "Does Paul have a friend?"

"No, and, fair warning, hands off. Got it?"

Sophie laughed before the line was disconnected.

"Who's Logan?" Finn asked.

"It's a bar about six blocks from here. A few of us from the newspaper hang out there when we can."

"Noisy?"

"Afraid so. Sorry."

Finn chuckled. "It won't be so bad if there are rewards involved."

Carrie smiled. "I imagine there will be more than a few."

"Then bring on the noise."

For the rest of the afternoon they simply hung out together while a medley of Christmas songs played in the background. It seemed they never ran out of things to talk about. And as promised, Finn gave her sections of his new book to read and critique. Carrie found it as good as, if not better than, *Alone* and told him so.

They left the condo around seven forty-five and with her arm tucked in Finn's they walked the six blocks to

Logan's. The noise was explosive the instant they entered the bar. Sophie and Bruce already had a table. Bruce worked for the newspaper, and he'd been dating Sophie for the last few months, following his divorce. According to Sophie, it wasn't a serious relationship, and after seeing them together a couple of times, Carrie had to agree.

The noise level made it nearly impossible to talk, but they managed by yelling across the table to one another. Finn ordered a beer. Sophie and Carrie had their favorite dirty martinis before another couple joined them. Introductions were made and a second round of drinks was ordered. Finn stayed close to her side and contributed to the conversation, although it was difficult with the bar so crowded. They left an hour later.

"I enjoyed meeting your friends," he commented when they were outside in the relative quiet of the street.

"But the crowds and the noise bothered you."

"Not bothered, exactly," he said, and reached for her hand. "I'm just not accustomed to it to that extent. We get plenty rowdy in Fairbanks ourselves, you know."

"But this is different."

He grinned and nodded. Soon they had their arms around each other as it started to snow again. They took a leisurely stroll down Michigan Avenue on the way back to Carrie's place. On a side street they walked past a bookstore, and *Alone* took up the entire window display. Finn paused and did a double take.

"How does it feel seeing that?" she asked.

He took his time answering. "I've seen it displayed before, but nothing like this. It leaves me feeling a little . . . I don't know, weird, I guess."

"A *good* weird, though, right?" She felt proud for him and for all that he'd accomplished, proud to be with him. Carrie knew the phenomenal sales of his book had shocked Finn. He didn't seem to understand what it was about his book that fascinated readers. When he'd submitted the manuscript, he'd been amazed at how quickly it'd sold. Then to have it shoot straight to the top of the bestseller lists and remain there for months on end was beyond the scope of his imagination.

"I can see your mind working," he said, and, leaning down, he kissed her brow. "I know what you're thinking."

"So you're a mind reader now."

"You'd love to write that article about me, wouldn't you?"

To deny it would be a falsehood, but to confess that she'd composed it a half-dozen times in her mind, even still had a rough draft on her laptop, would give him the wrong impression. "That's a moot point. I would never destroy the trust you have in me. I wouldn't submit a word until you gave me the approval to do so."

He was silent for a long time and then said, "Fair enough."

They held hands as he walked her to her condo and kissed her good night.

"Come upstairs with me?" she asked.

He shook his head. "I think I should go back to the hotel."

Carrie held on to his hand. "Is everything all right? You're not upset about anything, are you?"

Finn brought her back into his arms and hugged her close. "You're far too tempting, Carrie. If I came upstairs with you now, I wouldn't be leaving until morning, and we both know it."

Carrie went into her building with a happy, excited sense of anticipation and relief. She would see Finn tomorrow. He'd met her friends and not a one had even suspected her Seattle Paul was Finnegan Dalton.

# Chapter 12

"When is Paul leaving?" Sophie asked on Saturday afternoon. Finn was in her kitchen, fixing sandwiches for their lunch. Carrie had been bringing down dishes when her friend had called.

"His flight is scheduled for Monday. I mentioned our Christmas party, and I hope he'll be able to change his plans so he'll be staying for that." He'd used her laptop to see about alternate flights and to check his emails, but it didn't look promising that he'd be able to delay his return to Alaska.

"Do you think he might?"

"I don't know." The thought of him leaving filled her with dismay, but at the same time she appreciated that city life was completely foreign to him.

And she would need to return to work Monday morning and he'd be restless in the city, although there would be plenty for him to see and do.

"How come you left so early last night?" Sophie pressed.

"Too noisy," she explained, as she strolled into the kitchen. "It was difficult to hold a decent conversation, and Paul and I had been out and about all day."

"I have an idea," Sophie returned cheerfully, as if she was the most brilliant woman in the universe. "I'll have the two of you over for dinner this evening. I'll ask Bruce, and we'll have a small dinner party with just the four of us—nothing fancy."

"Good idea, but I've already got a roast in the Crock-Pot." A good portion of the leftover turkey had gone into the freezer, and she'd made up plates with turkey, stuffing, and the other side dishes to distribute to her neighbors who were widowers.

"Great," Sophie returned enthusiastically. "Then we'll come to your place. Does six work?"

Carrie glanced at Finn, knowing he could hear the conversation, and he shrugged as if to say it was her decision. "Sure. We'll see you then." Carrie would have preferred to spend the night with just her and Finn, but she had more or less been manipulated into agreeing. Setting her phone aside, she wrapped her arms around Finn's waist. "Are you sure you want to do this?" she asked. "I can call Sophie back and tell her we've changed our minds."

"It'll be fine. I liked your friends." He downplayed her concern, kissed her cheek, and brought their turkey-salad sandwiches to the table.

Sophie and Bruce arrived at six, bringing flowers and chocolate-dipped strawberries for dessert. Her friends wore matching Santa hats. The flowers became the centerpiece, and the meal was served. Conversation flowed smoothly throughout dinner. For obvious reasons, the answers to questions directed at Finn were vague. Sophie was the one who asked one question after another, almost as if she were conducting an interview. At one point, Carrie opened her mouth to stop her, an uneasy feeling filling her chest, but Finn pressed his hand over hers, reassuring her that all was fine.

Following the meal, Bruce and Finn went into the living room to watch a college football game while Sophie and Carrie cleared the table.

The instant they were out of earshot, Sophie hissed, "Who do you think you're kidding? That's Finn Dalton."

Just as she'd suspected when Sophie started hitting Finn with a barrage of questions, her friend had seen through their little masquerade.

Carrie started to explain when Sophie quickly cut her off. "Don't even try to deny it."

"All right, all right, yes, it's Finn. Paul is his middle name."

Sophie rolled her eyes. "Who did you think you were fooling, Carrie?"

"Do you remember," Carrie said, grabbing hold of her friend's forearm, "you said that Finn Dalton could be walking down the streets of Chicago and no one would even know it was him? Well, guess what, he is, and you're right, no one knows."

"Carrie, I'm worried about you. Surely you realize this relationship isn't going to work. Long-distance relationships rarely do. The two of you are night and day, oil and water."

"Well, to this point we seem to be coming along rather nicely," Carrie countered, unwilling to let her friend rain on her parade. Not for anything would Carrie give up on her and Finn.

"For the love of heaven, why haven't you written the article?" Sophie demanded. "We both know what that would mean to you and your career. You could have your choice of jobs with any newspaper. You're always talking about moving back to Seattle one day. This is your golden opportunity."

"The article is off the table." Carrie rinsed the dirty dishes and set them inside the dishwasher, not wanting to have this conversation. "I'd rather not discuss this, Sophie."

"Why can't you write it?" Sophie wasn't willing to let this go.

Carrie straightened and faced her friend head-on. "Finn asked me not to."

"What?" Sophie all but exploded.

Carrie hurriedly glanced around the wall that separated the kitchen from the living room to be sure Finn hadn't heard any part of this conversation. Both men appeared caught up in the football game. Sighing with relief, Carrie turned back to her friend.

"Keep your voice down, would you?"

"Sorry, but you need to think this through; give me one good reason why you aren't writing that article. Just one." She held up her finger and threatened to wag it with every word.

The answer should be obvious. "In case you hadn't figured it out, I'm in love with Finn."

"You barely know the guy," Sophie challenged.

"I know him well enough."

"Listen, Carrie, I realize you *think* you're in love, but you aren't. This is a classic case of wild infatuation. Opposites attract, right?" She didn't wait for a response. "You've gone bonkers for him, and it's understandable. He's not bad looking, and he seems to be a nice guy, but tell me, do you honestly see yourself picking berries out in the wilderness in order to survive?"

Sophie was right about one thing; Carrie couldn't see herself living her life in Finn's cabin, raising a family in such a limited environment. Still, she wasn't willing to give up Finn.

"What about your career?" Sophie challenged next.

"I can write anywhere."

"You can," Sophie reluctantly agreed. "You're smart and talented. But you can't seriously be considering giving up this golden opportunity."

Carrie lowered her voice to a whisper. "I won't betray Finn. I'm not that kind of person."

"I can't bear to see you make this sacrifice," Sophie insisted. "You'd be a fool not to take advantage of what you know about him."

Carrie refused to listen to this any longer. "Stop, Sophie. I said I'm not doing it, and I mean it. End of story."

Sophie gave a disgusted shake of her head. "Don't you see what he's doing?"

"What are you talking about? He trusts me, and I trust him."

"Aren't you afraid he might be using you?"

"Using me? For what?" The idea was so preposterous that Carrie nearly laughed out loud.

"To keep track of what you're doing so you won't write the article," Sophie explained.

Carrie shook her head, finding this conversation almost comical. "Finn isn't like that."

"Are you sure?" Sophie challenged. "Take my advice and admit that this relationship isn't going anywhere. If you hang on, you'll only be setting yourself up for heartache. I'm your friend, and I have your best interests at heart."

Carrie actually felt sorry for her. "You are getting to be such a cynic, Sophie. How can you say these things?"

"How can you be sure he isn't with you so that you won't write the article?" Sophie asked. "Against all odds, you found him. You know too much."

"Stop," Carrie insisted. "I don't want to hear it." She was finished with this conversation. She tossed the dish towel down on the counter, jerked the Christmas apron loose from her waist, and stuffed it in a drawer. "I'm done listening to you," she said.

Abruptly, she turned away from her friend, and to her shock she found Finn standing in the doorway.

Sophie cast her an apologetic glance, murmured, "Oops," and then scooted past Finn. "Hey, Bruce, time for us to leave."

"But the game . . ."

"You can watch it from my place."

Carrie waited until she heard the front door click closed. "How much of that did you hear?" she asked.

Finn had his arms crossed over his muscular chest. His frown compressed his forehead. "I heard enough."

"Don't be offended by Sophie. She doesn't know what she's talking about. She certainly doesn't know my heart."

"Don't be so sure."

"Finn . . ."

"You mean to say you never guessed what caused my change in attitude while we were in the cabin?"

"I . . ." She frowned. "No . . ."

"When you first arrived I was determined not to give you a single bit of information, and then you riled me to the point where I said far more than I ever intended. Very clever of you, by the way."

"I didn't mean . . . That wasn't my intention." He couldn't honestly believe that the argument about his mother had been prompted by anything other than exactly what it was. She hadn't been looking for a way to unearth his motivations so she could share them with the rest of the world. He couldn't actually believe that, could he?

"Despite my best efforts to keep you in the dark, it was clear you had enough on me to write ten articles if that was what you wanted," he continued.

Unwilling to trust his words, Carrie shook her head. "I don't believe you any more than I do Sophie. Are you telling me this has all been a game . . . you don't have any feelings for me?" She shook her head.

"Okay, sure. You're attractive and fun, and for a while I actually thought there might be something between us, but these last few days have shown me nothing permanent will ever come of this relationship." He looked almost apologetic. "I was perfectly content until you came into my life; I will be again, and so will you. We had a good run, but it's time we were realistic enough to accept that this relationship isn't good for either of us. It was always about the article."

He couldn't possibly mean what he was telling her. "Finn, please. You're overreacting. Sophie's like that. She makes assumptions she shouldn't. I would never betray your trust. Never."

He stared at her long and hard. "You're dying to write the article, aren't you? You as much as admitted it. An article on me would make your career."

"I don't care about that stupid article; what matters to me is you."

"Then you're lying." He wiped his hand across his face.

"I am not lying."

He exhaled slowly. "Carrie, I saw it on your laptop."

"What?" She slowly shook her head. "But that was before—" Abruptly, she stopped and sucked in her breath. She'd never deleted the rough draft of the article she'd written while in Alaska. It remained on her computer, nearly forgotten. Finn had used her laptop to check availability with the airlines and his emails. He must have seen it then. "Okay, yes, there's an article there, but did you look at the date? I wrote that while I was at the cabin before . . . before you asked me not to publish it."

Finn shook his head. "We're in over our heads. This isn't going to work. Sophie's comments should be a wake-up call to us both. She knows it, your mother knows it, and for that matter my mother, too. It's time for us to be honest, Carrie. This relationship is doomed. It always has been."

"Stop saying that. I'm not willing to give up on us. I love you, Finn." She threw her heart out to him and waited breathlessly for him to respond.

For the longest time all he did was stare at her. His shoulders sagged, and he released his breath in a long, slow exhale. "I'm sorry, Carrie. I don't love you."

"Now who's lying?" she asked, hiccupping on a half-sob. It felt as if the floor had started to pitch beneath her feet as though she were on board a ship, tossed about in a vicious storm at sea.

"Believe what you want."

His words hit her with a nearly physical impact. It felt as though he'd reached out and shoved her backward. Despite herself, she stumbled back several steps.

Although she recognized that it would do little good to argue with him, she made the effort. "What about the toaster?" she whispered, hardly able to speak because of the tightness in her throat. She might be able to believe him if she didn't know about the significance of the toaster. It meant far more to him than an antique. It'd been his way of telling her she was important to him. As important to him as his mother had been to his father.

"Ah, yes, the toaster. That was a rather brilliant move

on my part. I didn't know yet if you'd take my request seriously. I needed to do something that would have an effect on you, and I figured you'd ask my mother about it."

Her knees suddenly felt like they were about to collapse on her. She needed to sit down, and quickly.

Finn started for the door, briefly hesitated, and turned the knob.

"Take the Christmas present with you," she called after him, anger coming to rescue her pride in those final seconds.

"Keep it," he said on his way out the door, as if it meant nothing.

As if she meant nothing.

# Chapter 13

Carrie didn't even bother to go to bed that night or the next, sleeping in fits and starts, a few minutes at a time. She sat up on her sofa with a quilt her mother had lovingly crafted for her while she was in college. With its thick warmth wrapped around her shoulders, she tried to digest what had happened between her and Finn, and what would happen next—if anything. Try as she might, she couldn't make herself believe that the things he said had even the smallest semblance of truth.

At seven Monday morning she tossed aside the quilt, and although she was bone tired, she readied for work. Staring at her reflection, Carrie did her best to disguise the dark circles beneath her eyes, but with little success.

Sophie, who usually rushed into the office five minutes late, was already at her cubicle when Carrie arrived at her normal time. Her friend had left several messages, but Carrie hadn't answered her phone or responded to text messages.

Sophie didn't wait for Carrie to remove her hat and coat before she pounced on her, seeking information.

"What happened Saturday night after Bruce and I left?" she demanded. "Why didn't you answer any of my phone messages or texts?"

Carrie stared back blankly.

Sophie lowered her voice. "I feel terrible that Finn heard the things I said."

Fearing that if she said one word she would give in to the emotion that threatened to overwhelm her, Carrie simply shook her head.

"You have to tell me," Sophie pleaded. "Me and my big mouth. I'll never forgive myself. How could I be so stupid?"

Carrie swallowed against the tightening knot in her throat and gave an offhand shrug. "Apparently, you were right."

"Right?" Sophie's jaw dropped several inches. "Right about what?"

Bending over to turn on her computer, Carrie did her

best to sound nonchalant and disengaged. "You might as well say 'I told you so.' Finn and I are over."

Sophie's look of disbelief slowly evolved into a frown. "You're kidding, right?"

How Carrie wished she was. In answer, she shook her head. "Finn wanted to end it; he basically said the same thing you did, that we could never make it work, blah, blah, blah."

"Finn said that and you believed him? Listen, Carrie, I was wrong. Before I left I saw the way he looked at you. If a man ever looked at me like that, I'd be willing to give up chocolate and bear his children."

With all her heart, Carrie wanted to believe that was true, but she wasn't sure it even mattered. Finn was gone. Nevertheless, she was hanging on to that slender thread called hope, only in her case it was ragged hope.

Sophie pulled out a chair and sat down. "Anyone with two functioning brain cells could see he's nuts over you."

"I'd like to believe you, I really would, but he left shortly after you did, and I haven't heard from him since. Frankly I doubt that I will."

Sophie stiffened. "Fine, then write that article. He can't treat you like that."

Why was it everything went back to that stupid article?

"You're going to do it, aren't you? You'd be a fool not to."

Carrie didn't need to think about it. Undoubtedly, it was what Finn expected of her. "I don't want to talk about it." Instead, she reached for her mouse and clicked on an email.

"You've got to write it," Sophie insisted.

"No, I don't."

"Are you off your rocker?" Sophie stood and did a complete three-hundred-and-sixty-degree turn. "Someone call a medic; Carrie's losing her mind."

Carrie stopped her friend from making fools of them both. "Don't you understand that's exactly what Finn expects me to do?"

"Then give him what he wants," Sophie suggested. "That way you can both have what you want. Don't be an idiot, Carrie. This opportunity is one that comes along once or maybe twice in a career. This is your chance to prove yourself to Nash."

"I can't."

"Why not?"

"Because Finn loves me." It was the only scenario that made sense to Carrie. He had vehemently denied it, but Carrie refused to accept that. For two nights she'd mulled over his words, and ultimately she chose not to believe them. She couldn't feel the things she did if it'd all been a lie.

"Where is Finn now?" Sophie asked. "Let me talk some sense into him."

"Sophie—" Carrie really didn't feel like discussing this now.

"Is he still in Chicago?" Sophie asked, cutting her off.

Carrie shook her head. "He's gone."

"Back to Alaska?"

Carrie didn't know, and so she shrugged. It didn't matter. She was confident that no matter where he was, Alaska or Timbuktu, he was as miserable as she.

"What happens now?" Sophie asked, showing signs of sympathy. "This is dreadful, just dreadful. I don't think I can bear it."

Again, Carrie answered with a lift of her shoulders. "I've spent the better part of the last two days and nights going over a variety of scenarios. I have to believe Finn will have a change of heart."

"You mean he'll come back for you?"

"No . . . he won't do that." That wouldn't be his way.

"I don't understand," Sophie said, speaking softly now.

"He's going to regret the lie that he doesn't care, doesn't love me, and so he'll make it up to me the only way he can."

"And how's that?"

"He'll ask me to be the one to break the story on him."

"Of course." Sophie vaulted to her feet and clapped her hands. "Of course. It's brilliant. And you'll do it, and then . . ."

"No."

Sophie froze. "No?"

"No," Carrie repeated. "I'm going to refuse."

"Stop." Sophie planted her hands on top of her head. "This is like a chess game, and I'm losing track of the moves. If he wants you to write the piece, then why won't you do it?"

"Because if I refuse it will force his hand."

Sophie scratched the side of her head as though puzzled. "I don't follow."

"Finn wants me to publish something about him because it will salve his conscience. It's the one way he has of apologizing, of letting me know he loves me. But I won't do it, because it's the only way I can think to let him know I love him. It's the one thing I can do to tell him my feelings haven't changed."

Sophie sat back in the chair. "You're losing me, girlfriend."

It was a gamble for sure, Carrie realized. And until she got word from Finn, she would need to keep silent. There was a chance, of course, that she was completely wrong and she would never hear from him again. For now, it was a waiting game.

The first week of December passed. Long, torturous days in which there was complete silence from Finn. Somehow Carrie got through her and Sophie's little Christmas gathering. She managed to smile and even laugh now and again. It was a great party, everyone said, and Carrie was grateful she was able to pull it off. The only person who seemed to notice that Carrie's spirits were low was Sophie.

"I'm having a hard time dealing with this guilt," her friend confessed. "I feel like I'm to blame. I look at you and I want to cry. You're so miserable, and it's all my fault."

Carrie did her best to reassure her friend. "Don't worry. These matters have a way of working out how they're meant to be." While she might have sounded confident, Carrie was anything but.

Another week of silence followed. Carrie lost weight. Sleep felt like a luxury.

On Friday a few days before Christmas, just before quitting time, the office threw a small party. Carrie was scheduled to fly back to Seattle in the morning, to be with her family, and she was getting ready to head home to pack when she got word that Nash wanted to speak to her in his office.

She knocked against his door and stepped inside. Without looking away from his computer screen, he motioned for her to take a seat.

Carrie complied.

"I just got off the phone with some New York publicity woman," he said, frowning at her as if seeing her for the first time. "How is it that you know Finn Dalton?"

"Who says I know Finn?" she parried with a question of her own.

"You said you were determined to find him, as I recall."

"So I did." She folded her hands in her lap, afraid the trembling would give her away.

"Well, congratulations. It seems you looked under the right rock, because this PR person called to tell me Finn Dalton is ready to let someone interview him. The surprising part is that he requested you, and he claims you already know everything there is to know. He's requested you write the piece."

Carrie's eyes drifted shut. This was exactly the news she'd been waiting to hear. She'd been right. Finn had offered her the assignment. A sense of release and joy rushed through her. He was as much as telling her that he loved her. She pressed her hand to her mouth, fearing she was about to break into sobs.

"I can see you're pleased. I'd be crying with joy, too. I don't know what you did, but congratulations. This is one of the biggest coups this newspaper has had in a long time. How soon can you write the piece? If possible, I'd like to have it for the weekend edition."

"Sorry, Nash, Mr. Dalton's publisher is going to need to find someone else."

"What?" Nash nearly came out of his chair. "Is this a joke? If so, I'm not laughing."

Now wasn't the time to back down. Carrie had to remain strong. As badly as she ached to give in, she couldn't do it. "I hate to disappoint you, but you'll need to find someone else."

Nash shook his head. "The publisher insists you have to be the one. No one else."

It was exactly as she'd calculated. "Sorry." She blinked back tears.

The hard-core newsman glared at her. "Your job is on the line, Ms. Slayton. This newspaper can't afford to let this opportunity slip by. I'm giving you twenty-four hours to change your mind."

Losing her job was an aspect of this decision that she hadn't considered. Carrie swallowed hard and bit into her lower lip. "It won't matter if it's twenty-four hours or twenty-four days. I'm not going to change my mind."

Disgusted, Nash shook his head.

"I'm leaving in the morning for Seattle to see my family." It seemed her Christmas break would now be spent seeking another job. It was a steep price to pay to prove her love to Finn, but she wouldn't back down.

"Go have Christmas with your family," Nash said, motioning for her to leave his office. "But take this time to think about what I said. I'm serious, Carrie. Write the article and keep your job. Otherwise, you can clear out your desk when you return."

"And if I write the article, what about your promise to me?"

"What promise?"

"Any assignment I want, any department." He hadn't said it quite like that; still, it wouldn't do any harm to press her point.

Nash hesitated and then sighed. "It's negotiable."

Sophie was waiting for her at Carrie's desk when she returned. Her friend had glittery silver tinsel wrapped around her neck like a Hawaiian lei. "So, what did Nash want?"

When she told her about the call from the New York publicist, Sophie leaped up and gave a loud cheer. "This is exactly what you said would happen."

"This is the way I *hoped* it would play out."

"So?" Sophie said eagerly, shifting her arms back and forth, "what's the next move?"

"I don't know."

"What do you mean you don't know? I thought you had this all planned out."

How Carrie wished that were true. She knew what she had to do, but the rest was up to Finn.

The next day Carrie sat at the O'Hare Airport gate, waiting to board her flight to Seattle, when her cell chirped. She didn't recognize the number but saw that it was an Alaska prefix.

"Hello," she answered hesitatingly.

"Carrie, this is Sawyer O'Halloran."

"Sawyer?" She couldn't imagine why he would be calling her, unless something had happened to Finn. She gripped hold of the phone with both hands, instantly alarmed. "Is everything all right? Has Finn been hurt?"

"Yes . . . He isn't in the hospital or anything, if that's what you're wondering. What happened between the two of you, anyway?"

Carrie relaxed a bit. "You'll need to ask him about that."

"You're joking, right? He hasn't been himself since he returned from Chicago. I've never seen him like this. He disappeared for a couple of days, showed up drunk as a coyote, which is surprising, because he isn't much of a drinker. He isn't talking to anyone—well, other than me, but it's difficult to understand what he's saying. Furthermore, he isn't eating or sleeping."

Carrie exhaled and whispered into the small receiver. "Frankly, I'm not doing much better myself."

"You two had a falling out?"

"You could say that."

"Listen, before we go any further, Finn doesn't know I'm contacting you. If he finds out about this, he'll have my head."

"How'd you get my personal phone number?"

"Easy. I waited until he passed out and then checked his cell."

"He was that drunk?" This didn't sound anything like

Finn. It didn't make her feel any better knowing that he was miserable. All Carrie wanted was for this foolishness to be over.

"No, he wasn't drunk, but practically dead on his feet. I don't know the last time he slept. He kept mumbling something about giving you a shot at what you wanted, and you rejecting that. Don't know what that's about, but I figure you must."

Carrie simply shook her head. "If he wants to talk to me, all he needs to do is call."

"I'm not telling him that."

At this point, Carrie suspected Finn wasn't listening to advice from anyone.

"I have a feeling this all goes back to that article you wanted to publish. The one Finn asked you not to write."

"I'm afraid so. At first he was adamant I not write the piece, and now it seems he's had a change of heart. He's giving me what he thinks I want, but it isn't. What I want is him."

The line went silent. "I'm confused. He's giving you this opportunity because he loves you and you're turning it down because you love him? Have I got that right?"

"You do." Her flight was announced, and the boarding process had already started. "Listen, Sawyer, I need to get off the phone, but I want you to tell Finn something for me, if you would."

"I'm not letting him know we had this conversation. I value my head, which he'd bite off if he got so much as an inkling that I've contacted you."

"Fine, I understand, but if the opportunity comes up and he finds out we chatted, tell him that before I will agree to write a single word, he will need to sit down with me face-to-face; otherwise, it's no deal."

"That's your final answer?" Sawyer wanted to know.

"Yes."

Carrie disconnected the call and felt better than she had in almost three weeks.

# Chapter 14

Carrie's flight from Chicago landed at Sea-Tac Airport on time. It would be good to be with family over the Christmas holiday. She needed the comfort of their acceptance and love. Not a moment passed when Finn wasn't in the forefront of her mind.

She exited the plane and automatically reached for her cell, turning it on. Either her mother or father would be waiting in the cell-phone waiting area for her text message. As soon as it powered up, she typed in the information that she'd landed safely, and then headed toward the exit signs. She would go directly to baggage claim and meet them at the curb for pickup.

Dragging her carry-on behind her, she was following

her fellow passengers onto the escalator when her phone beeped, indicating she had a text message. Assuming it was one of her parents, she didn't immediately check. About halfway up, she glanced at her phone and saw that the text was from Finn. It shook her up so badly that she dropped the phone. Carrie watched in horror as it went tumbling down the escalator steps. "Please, someone grab that for me!" she cried out in a panic.

"Got it," a woman at the bottom shouted back to her.

As soon as Carrie reached the top, she hurriedly circled around and leaped onto the opposite escalator, racing down the steps, unwilling to stand and wait. The woman remained at the bottom and handed the cell back to her.

"Thank you," Carrie whispered, grabbing hold of it. "Thank you so much."

Her heart raced at a frantic speed as she opened Finn's text.

Why won't you write the article?

Her fingers moved in a blur as she typed her response. I would be happy to.

Good.

Once you give me a face-to-face interview.

His response was immediate. Not going to happen.

Then get someone else. She didn't expect Finn to be

thrilled with her stipulation. Seeing her again was the last thing he wanted, because it was sure to be difficult to answer her questions, and, even more so, to send her away.

She waited for a response, but none came.

Having collected her bag, Carrie was standing in the cold outside the airport, waiting to be picked up by her mother, when she heard the ping indicating Finn had responded. Why are you so stubborn?

An involuntary smile came over her as she rushed to answer. Because you lied. You love me.

Finn didn't deny or confirm her text, not that she'd expected he would. After a couple of moments, Carrie placed her phone inside her purse. The ache in her heart was back, stronger than ever. This could quite possibly be the last communication she might ever have with Finn. The thought sent her Christmas spirits spiraling downward.

Her mother pulled up to the airport curb, and after sticking her bags in the backseat, Carrie climbed inside the vehicle.

"I'm so glad you're home," her mother said, and they briefly hugged.

"I am, too," Carrie assured her. They drove off, heading to the family home, where her brother, his wife, and his children would be waiting. Soon they'd all be gathered around the table, and there would be laughter and conversation. Finn had never known this, and Carrie hungered to share her family with him.

"You okay, honey?" her mother asked, as they merged into the heavy freeway traffic. "You don't look so well. It's Finn, isn't it?"

Carrie nodded.

"How much weight have you lost?"

Carrie shrugged. "A few pounds is all."

Reaching over, her mother gave Carrie's hand a gentle squeeze. "Mark my words, it will all work out."

Carrie desperately wanted that to be true. Everything seemed so hopeless at the moment.

"Time is the great healer," her mother assured her.

She'd spent an hour on the phone with her mother shortly after her breakup with Finn, pouring out all her hurt and fears. Patty Slayton hadn't offered empty reassurances or reminded Carrie of her own concerns over this relationship; instead, she'd simply listened. At the end she'd said, "You really do love him, don't you?"

"Oh, yes." There was no doubt in Carrie's mind. Finn Dalton owned her heart. He carried it with him, and now the question, the real question, was what he intended to do with it.

"We're just glad you're home for the holidays," her mother said, pulling her back into the present.

"So am I." Carrie didn't mention that she might be returning to Seattle on a more permanent basis. For the first time since she'd spoken to Nash, she actually considered caving in. That was what Finn wanted her to do in an effort to ease his conscience. He could break her heart and then walk away without guilt because he'd done her a good turn. Writing that blasted article was what everyone hoped she'd do.

"I need to run an errand in the morning," Carrie casually mentioned once she was home and had emptied her suitcase. Dinner was over and her brother and family had returned to their home. "Do you mind if I borrow the car?" she asked her parents.

"You going to run off to Alaska?" her father asked.

"Nick Slayton," her mother hissed in a low, warning breath.

"Well, if Carrie is going to break up with Finn Dalton, why can't she do it after we have a chance to meet him?"

Both her mother and Carrie ignored the comment.

"I doubt very much that I'll be going to Alaska," Carrie said.

"Of course you can take the car." Her mother cast her

a questioning glance. "I don't have any plans for the morning."

"I shouldn't be gone more than an hour or two," Carrie assured her.

First thing the next morning, Carrie contacted Finn's mother and they set a time to meet. Joan had the front door open before Carrie had reached the end of the short walkway.

The older woman held open the screen door. They briefly hugged before Joan brought Carrie into the house. Her tree was up and decorated with festive ornaments, and her fireplace mantel displayed a wooden Nativity scene. Joan indicated that Carrie should take a seat on the sofa. Finn's mother had a teapot and two cups out, along with a plate of decorated sugar cookies.

"Finn used to help me decorate the cookies every Christmas," she said as they sat next to each other on the sofa. "He enjoyed it, although his father feared I was turning him into a sissy. My goodness, the boy was only four years old."

Joan handed her a cup of freshly poured tea, which Carrie accepted, holding on to the tiny saucer with one hand and the teacup with the other.

"Have you heard from my son?" Joan asked.

"Just briefly." There'd been nothing since their quick text exchanges late yesterday afternoon.

"It sounds like Finn is as stubborn as his father."

Carrie was afraid that was the case.

Joan exhaled as though emotionally bracing herself for what was coming. "You brought Paul's wedding band back to me?"

"Yes. I'm so sorry. I tried."

"I know, dear. I should never have put you in such an awkward position."

Carrie disagreed. "I doubt I could have convinced anyone to fly me to Finn's cabin without it, so the ring served a purpose." She dug it out of her purse, and with regret returned it to Finn's mother, feeling like she'd failed her.

Joan's eyes revealed her disappointment. "I so hoped . . ."

"I know; I did, too."

"I'm confident Paul went to his grave loving me. Unfortunately, pride prevented him from letting me know he wanted me back. He was unwilling to compromise. It could only be his way."

Carrie feared Joan might be right and Finn was like his father. He, too, would be willing to walk away from her and not look back.

They sipped their tea in silence for several moments while Carrie gathered her thoughts. "I'd appreciate your help with something."

"Of course."

Carrie reached into the bag she'd brought along with her. "I need you to tell me what this is." She brought out the Christmas gift Finn had left under her Christmas tree. Unable to wait any longer, Carrie had unwrapped his gift before she left Chicago, but she didn't have a clue as to what it might be. It was a narrow stick of what appeared to be fossilized ivory and was about twenty inches in length.

The night before, Carrie's father had taken a look at it and shook his head. He didn't have an answer for her.

Joan reached for the object and released a soft "Oh, my."

"What is it?" Carrie asked.

Joan reverently ran her hand down the piece, and then raised her eyes to Carrie's. "My son gave you this for Christmas?"

"Yes. What can you tell me about it?"

Joan nodded. "It's an oosik."

"Which is?" This wasn't helping.

"It's a walrus penis bone."

Carrie gasped. "A what?"

Joan laughed at the look that came over Carrie. "Leave it to my son."

"He gave me a toaster and a walrus penis bone?"

"This one is rather rare, though, if it's the same one Paul got all those years ago from an elderly Alaskan native."

"An oosik?" Carrie repeated, the word unfamiliar on her tongue.

"This one is a fossilized baculum and comes from an extinct walrus. They're highly collectible for Alaskan art. It was one of Paul's most prized possessions. At the time, and remember, this was many years ago, it was valued at around twenty thousand dollars."

"Why would Finn give it to me?" She wanted to clasp it to her breast, but that wouldn't bring Finn back.

"Isn't it obvious, my dear? He loves you."

It was too valuable, and it clearly held sentimental value to Joan. "I can't keep this," she said sadly, her mind made up. "I'd rather you take it."

Automatically, Joan shook her head. "Finn wanted you to have it."

"Please," Carrie whispered. "It should stay with you. And if by chance Finn and I . . ." Her voice caught, and she had to stop talking for fear her emotions might overwhelm her. "If Finn and I," she repeated, "manage to get back together, then you can save it to give to one of your grandchildren."

Joan's eyes filled with unshed tears, and she slowly nodded.

Deep down, Carrie believed she wouldn't hear from Finn again. She'd played her hand, laid down her cards, and her ploy had failed. Finn was unwilling to meet her face-to-face for an interview or anything else. He couldn't look her in the eye and say the things he had to her while in her kitchen, and they both knew it.

Christmas Eve day Carrie helped her mother get everything ready for their annual Christmas buffet. Instead of the big traditional dinner, complete with turkey and stuffing plus all the fixings, her mother served a multitude of longtime family favorites: several salads, casseroles, fried chicken, deviled eggs, and a ham, plus a wide variety of desserts.

On Christmas Day, friends and family would stop by to partake. Carrie always enjoyed this special time working in the kitchen with her mother. It seemed the most important discussions of her life had taken place in front of the stove or the refrigerator.

Carrie sliced the cooked potatoes for the potato salad,

her father's favorite, when her mother unexpectedly came to her and hugged her. "I know how hard this year has been for you, honey. Your heart is aching."

"I love him, Mom."

"Talking about him might help. Do you want to tell me what it is that you find so compelling about Finn Dalton?"

Discussing her feelings was exactly what Carrie needed. Everyone else seemed to tiptoe around anything having to do with Finn, afraid to bring up any reference to him. Carrie realized they were simply looking to protect her, but Finn had become the subject everyone had chosen to ignore.

"He's not like any man I've ever known," she told her mother. "He's resourceful and resilient, quick-witted and generous. He has the most wonderful subtle sense of humor. I can laugh with him more than I have with anyone else I've ever met. And he's incredibly intelligent. Everyone looks at us and all they see are the differences, but beneath it all we share the same values, the same sense of what's important. He told me over Thanksgiving how much he envies me my family, and if he ever had one of his own he'd make sure he would be the kind of husband and father my own dad has been." She paused, remembering the night they'd stood out and gazed at the heavens. "And while he'd never openly admit it, he loves Christmas. He helped me put up decorations without a word of complaint. He has a Nativity set from when he was a kid and admitted he sets it up every year. I don't think anyone else knows he does that." She smiled, remembering how she'd amused herself while he was gone from the cabin. "When I was with him in Alaska, I hung paper snowflakes from the ceiling of his cabin."

Her mother laughed. "I can only imagine what he thought of that."

"The truth is, Mom, I don't think he minded. For all I know, they are still up. They should have been stars, though, instead of snowflakes."

"Oh?"

"After the snowstorm had died down, we stood outside under the stars. Oh, Mom, you can't imagine how beautiful the night sky is in Alaska. All those stars— I've never seen anything that could compare to it. They were like fairy dust sprinkled across the heavens. I think it was on that starry night that I realized I was falling in love with Finn."

He'd felt it, too, Carrie knew. Everything had changed between them from that moment on. It'd been magical, wondrous, with his arms around her. He would never admit it, but those few minutes under the stars had shaken Finn. They'd deeply affected her as well.

"What about his family?" her mother asked.

"His mother is wonderful, and she loves her son and wants to be reunited with him. Finn is struggling with that." He'd never come out and say as much, but Carrie could sense it from little things that had happened, things he'd said and done. He wanted to ignore the fact that he had a mother, but try as he might, he still cared.

"He seems to be struggling with a great deal at the moment," her mother said.

"He is," Carrie agreed, and like her, he was hurting. She wondered if he thought about the things they'd discussed when he'd been with her over Thanksgiving. He'd told her his dreams and she'd shared her own, and while they lived in different worlds, they'd found common ground and a deep connection.

Perhaps she was being unreasonable about all this, Carrie mused. If Finn wanted to clear his conscience and be done with the relationship all in one fell swoop, she shouldn't stand in his way. This was what he wanted. No one could write about him the way she could. Carrie suspected that outside of Sawyer, few knew Finn better than she did.

"I'm afraid, Mom—afraid I will never love anyone as deeply as I do Finn."

"Oh, honey, you can't see it now, but in time you'll be able to remember him without pain. Love doesn't die."

"Loving someone shouldn't hurt like this."

"True," her mother whispered, and placed her arm around Carrie's shoulders. "And in the future, when you're able to look back, I promise you it won't hurt as intensely as it does now. You'll feel sad for what might have been, but the pain will be gone."

Later, after all the salads had been made and the dishes washed and put away, Carrie retreated to her childhood bedroom. She sat on her bed, rehashing the conversation with her mother. It'd been a good talk, and while she didn't hold out much hope, she couldn't help reaching for her phone, longing for a text or call from Finn.

There wasn't one.

In a couple of hours, Carrie would be joining her family for Christmas Eve services at their church. She wasn't much in the mood, but she wouldn't disappoint her family by staying home. Church was exactly where she needed to be. This was Christmas, with or without Finn.

Before she could change her mind, she reached for her phone and sent a brief message to him.

Merry Christmas. Look at the stars tonight and remember me.

# Chapter 15

Christmas morning, Carrie woke and waited for the dark cloud that seemed to hang over her head to return. It didn't. She sat up in bed with a deep sense of peace. She'd followed her heart, and while she would always love Finn, she was ready to move forward. Today was Christmas, and she wasn't going to allow her current sorrows to mar the day.

Hearing movement in the kitchen, she knew her parents were up. They enjoyed their morning ritual of having coffee together. How fortunate she was to have parents who continued to love and care for each other. Carrie didn't want to disturb their special time, and so she gathered her clothes together and headed into her tiny bathroom for a shower.

Her mother noticed the change in Carrie's attitude right away. "I feel better," she said, hugging both her parents. "I'm going to be okay now."

"I know you will be," her mother said, hugging her back.

"I'd like to give that young man a piece of my mind," her father insisted. "If I had my way, I'd string Finn Dalton up by his thumbs for hurting my little girl."

"Oh, Daddy," Carrie chided, loving him for wanting to make things right for his daughter.

By noon her brother and his family had stopped by for breakfast on their way to his in-laws'. All the gifts had been opened, and Carrie was busy in the kitchen, helping her mother get everything set up for their buffet, when the doorbell chimed.

"That'll be Charlie," her father called out from the other room.

"Uncle" Charlie Hines was a longtime family friend who'd remained a bachelor. He made sure he was one of the first to stop by for the feast, claiming he never ate better than Christmas Day at Nick and Patty's.

Carrie and her mother had barely gotten the food displayed on the table.

"That Charlie," her mother said under her breath,

setting down a pitcher of water. "He comes earlier every year."

"It's probably the only decent dinner he eats," Carrie added, as she followed her mother out to greet him.

Only it wasn't Charlie who stood in the middle of the living room. Instead, it was Joan and Finn. Mother and son. Together.

Thankfully, Carrie had set down the last of the salads from the kitchen; otherwise, there would be lettuce and heaven knew what else tossed all across the carpet.

"Merry Christmas," Joan said. "I hate to intrude, but I brought someone with me I thought you might like to see."

Carrie's mouth had gone completely dry. She couldn't utter a word—not a single, solitary word.

"You're not intruding," Carrie's mother assured her, as she stepped forward to clasp the other woman's hand. "I'm Patty Slayton, Carrie's mother."

"Joan Dalton Reese, Finn's mother."

The two women hugged, and the introductions continued as Nick came in.

Finn's intense gaze settled on Carrie. Everyone seemed to be watching them. Carrie wanted to welcome them both, but couldn't because she found it impossible to speak. Never, in all her life, had she seen a more welcome sight than Finnegan Dalton standing in the middle of her parents' living room early Christmas afternoon. He seemed to fill up the space, his eyes boring into hers, waiting, questioning.

Not knowing what else to do, Carrie did what seemed to be the only sensible thing—she rushed across the room and launched herself into Finn's arms.

He caught her around the waist, lifting her off the floor. And then they were kissing. It felt as if the last few weeks boiled down to this one hungry, passionate kiss. It was as if they were starved for each other.

Carrie's hands framed his face, his beautiful bearded face. The beard wasn't as thick as before, but his whiskers were back. His beautiful, dark whiskers. It didn't matter that they had an audience or that Joan was chatting animatedly with her parents. The only important thing was Finn, the man she loved.

"Come into the family room," her mother was saying to Joan. "I have the feeling these two might appreciate a few minutes alone."

"Before he leaves I want to talk to that young man," her father objected.

"Not to worry," Joan assured him. "I believe Finn wants to talk to you, too."

And then it was just the two of them, as her parents and Joan left the room.

Finn lowered her until her feet were on the floor. Carrie kept her hands on his face, unable to stop looking at him. "You're here," she whispered. "You're actually here."

She led him to the sofa and then sat on his lap. His eyes were eating her up as if he'd been without water for far too long and she was a freshwater spring. "What have you done to me, Carrie Slayton?"

"Loved you," she returned.

"I gave you the career opportunity of a lifetime, and you turned it down." He shook his head as if even now he couldn't believe that she'd refused. Carrie found it hard to believe herself, only it had been necessary.

"My career isn't nearly as important as you are."

"This is crazy, Carrie. We have everything going against us. You live in Chicago, and I'm in Alaska . . ."

"I'll move," she said, cutting him off, and then pulled his mouth to hers and kissed him in a way that left them both weak and breathless. "We'll make it work," she insisted, her eyes still closed. She reveled in the taste and feel of him holding her. It'd been far too long since she'd been in his arms. She hadn't realized how badly she'd missed his touch.

"When you kiss me like that you make me believe."

"Good." She couldn't keep from touching him. Her hands roamed over his neck and shoulders, savoring the feel of him. "You've reconciled with your mother?"

He rubbed his hand over his eyes. "I'd pushed you out of my life. I'd been alone before, but not like this, and then I remembered something you'd said."

"Me?"

"Yes, you." He leaned down and kissed the tip of her nose. "I asked if my mother needed anything, and you said the only thing she really needed was her son."

"I was with her yesterday morning." Carrie couldn't believe Joan would hold back the news that she'd heard from Finn.

"I didn't call her before I came. I wasn't sure I had the courage to go through with it until I pulled up to her house late last night. I told myself I was coming to Seattle to make amends with her, but the real reason was I couldn't stay away from you. Not for another minute."

"Oh, Finn, this is the best Christmas of my life."

He couldn't seem to stop staring at her. "You gave my mother the oosik," he commented.

Carrie lowered her gaze. "I couldn't keep anything that valuable, Finn. It was more important that she have it than me."

"But what you said to her," he returned, frowning.

Carrie couldn't remember anything specific. "What do you mean?"

"That if the two of us were to get back together, she should save it for one of her grandchildren."

Carrie relaxed and smiled. The warm, happy feeling that had come over her that morning intensified. Had her heart known Finn was close? she wondered. She hardly knew how else to explain this sensation.

"You want it all, don't you? Marriage, children, a career."

"Of course. It's what you want, too, Finn."

He closed his eyes and nodded. "Yes," he whispered, "more than I ever knew, although I didn't realize it until I met you."

Carrie braced her forehead against his. "It doesn't matter to me where we settle—Alaska, Washington, Illinois—because my home is wherever you are."

He hugged her even closer. "I thought I could walk away from you, but I couldn't. I've never needed anyone the way I need you. I felt alone, truly alone, for the first time. Then you sent me that text, reminding me about the night we viewed the stars. You asked me to remember you. Did you honestly believe forgetting you was even possible? I fell in love with you that starry night."

"That was the night when I realized I was falling in love with you, too," she confessed. It had been that special moment, gazing up at the heavens, when she'd felt that connection with Finn, unaware that from that moment forward their futures would be forever linked. It seemed as though the heavens had smiled down on them both and offered them a blessing.

"I can't believe you're here," Carrie whispered, worshipping him with her eyes, loving him so much it felt as though her heart were about to crack wide open.

"Oh, yes, I'm here and I'm not going away. I doubt Sawyer is talking to me any longer, and even Hennessey looks at me with disgust." He studied her, his gaze delving into hers. "I hardly know myself any longer."

"Oh, Finn, I love you so much."

He brushed the hair from her forehead. "Answer me truthfully, Carrie. Would you seriously consider resigning from your job with the newspaper?"

This wasn't a difficult question. Carrie nodded. Her ultimate goal had always been to eventually return to Seattle. "I don't have to work for a newspaper to be a writer. I'd even be happy freelancing from home."

He hugged her close. "My home is wherever you are. I think to be fair to us both, we can divide our time between Seattle and Alaska."

"You'd be willing to do that?"

Finn smiled down on her and kissed her again. "I want the opportunity to get to know my mother, and this will give you a chance to be close to your own family. We'll make it work, Carrie."

"My home is with you and with Hennessey, and then later, of course, we'll be adding to the family."

His head came back up. "You want another dog?"

Carrie slapped his chest. "No, silly. Children."

"Oh, yes," he said with a chuckle.

Carrie nestled her head beneath his chin. "Things are right between you and your mother?" Although she hadn't been able to take her eyes off Finn, Carrie had noticed the happiness that seemed to radiate off Joan. It seemed both Carrie and Joan were having the best Christmases of their lives.

"You were right about her. She's never stopped loving me."

"You seem to have that effect on women."

He brought her mouth close to his. "Certain women, at any rate."

"This woman."

Finn spread nibbling kisses down the side of her neck. "This man loves this woman."

"Good, because this is just the beginning for us. And this time it's for keeps."

"For keeps," Finn repeated. He was willing to admit he'd been a fool. He'd assumed he'd be able to walk away from Carrie and not look back. At the time, it'd seemed the prudent choice. He knew when he found the article on her laptop that Carrie had never intended to submit it. Finding it gave him all the excuse he needed to break it off. Only she'd called his bluff. She'd forced him to lie. He wasn't proud of the things he'd said to Carrie. At the time, it had seemed necessary. Finn had believed that it would be tough the first couple of days but within a short amount of time he'd be over her.

Wrong.

Miserable didn't even begin to describe his feelings. He felt lost, cast adrift with nothing to anchor him. Before Carrie had entered his life, everything seemed perfectly fine. He'd been content. Happy, even—and perhaps he was.

Then she was dumped into his well-ordered existence —no thanks to Sawyer O'Halloran—and everything changed. All at once he became aware of the dark shadows in what had once been light, the isolation he'd accepted rather than deal with the past and his parents' divorce. At first he assumed he could let her go, and he later realized he was making the same mistake as his father with his unwillingness to compromise. His father had been determined to stand his ground. If Joan loved him, she would accept his terms, and as a result he'd ended up lonely and bitter. Finn refused to repeat history. He loved Carrie, and if loving her meant spending part of the year in Seattle, then that was a small sacrifice in order to make her his wife. In order to make her happy.

His thoughts returned to his ridiculous efforts to sever the relationship. Carrie knew him far too well, had refused to believe he didn't love her. How easily she saw through his ploy. She'd read him perfectly. If that wasn't bad enough, she'd been unwilling to settle for his token apology by giving her the opportunity to write the article about him that everyone seemed to want.

This woman could be stubborn. It didn't help matters that she held his heart in the palm of her hand. Still, he fought it; still, he assumed he could go on without her. What a laugh that turned out to be.

It wasn't only Carrie, either. In all the years since his mother had walked out, not once had Finn felt the need to connect with her again. She'd left him and his father. Pride demanded that he have nothing more to do with her, despite her repeated efforts to reach out to him.

Feeling alone and lost, Finn had to accept that as difficult as it was to admit, he needed his mother. His children would need their grandmother.

Carrie wanted children. The thought both thrilled and terrified him.

"You've got a funny look," she said, gazing up at him, frowning slightly.

Finn kissed her again, and a sense of happiness and joy filled him until it felt as if he could soar. "We're going to be just fine."

"Yes, I know," Carrie agreed.

Her parents and his mother came back into the room, and Carrie scooted off his lap. They stood and he slipped his arm around her waist.

Her mother's eyes were moist with tears, and she held her fingers against her lips, watching the two of them.

"Are you going to love our Carrie?" Nick Slayton asked.

"Dad!" she protested, clearly embarrassed.

"With all my heart," Finn promised, keeping her close against his side.

"That's good enough for me." Nick thrust out his hand for Finn to shake. "Welcome to the family."

The two men clasped hands, and their gazes held for an extra-long moment as understanding passed between the two of them.

Oh, yes, this was definitely going to be the best Christmas of Finn Dalton's life.

Read on for the first chapter of Debbie's
new book *Blossom Street Brides*, to be published by
Arrow in March 2014

# *Chapter 1*

Lauren Elliott had received the most depressing news of her life.

Her sister was pregnant.

Her *younger* sister.

Oh, she was happy and excited for Carol, but mingled in with the joy was an undeniable sense of envy. The fact that Carol was about to become a mother shouldn't come as a shock—her sister and Jason had been married for two years, after all. Lauren loved her sister, and Jason would make a wonderful father. What bothered her was the fact that at age thirty-four, Lauren was still unmarried. *Single.* Oh, how she'd come to hate that word.

Walking down Blossom Street, Lauren buried her

hands deep into the pockets of her fawn-colored rain jacket. Tulips and crocuses bloomed in the flowerpots that hung from the streetlights and the scent of roses, lilacs, and camellias followed her as she walked past Susannah's Garden, the flower shop.

Lauren kept her head down as she mulled over this latest development. This was it. The end of her rope. The line in the sand. She was finished waiting for Todd to give her an engagement ring. A year earlier she'd had the DTR—Defining the Relationship—talk with Todd and he'd assured her that marriage was definitely part of their future. Only he wasn't in a financial position to make the leap just yet. He'd suggested they give it time, and she'd reluctantly agreed. That was twelve months ago, and frankly her patience was shot. She'd dated the popular local television newscaster for three years and it was time to own up to the truth. If Todd was sincere about wanting her for his wife, then she would have had a diamond on her ring finger long before now.

Clearly Todd enjoyed their relationship just the way it was, and in some ways so did she. Todd was fun and smart, and she liked being with him. Because of his job, Lauren frequently accompanied him to high-profile social events. As a result, she was able to mingle with some of the city's elite, and it didn't hurt that many of these socialites came to John Michael Jewelers, where she worked, for their jewelry needs.

Lauren passed A Good Yarn and the window display instantly caught her attention. She stopped to give it a look and shook her head. Wouldn't you know it, the display in the yarn store's window was a baby blanket.

A beautiful baby blanket knit in lovely pastel colors. Lauren wanted to groan. She loved her sister, but there'd always been a friendly rivalry between them. More laid-back of the two, Lauren didn't have big career ambitions, whereas Carol worked as a program designer for a large software company out of California. She'd married her college sweetheart and seemed to have the perfect life.

Lauren had dropped out of college after a couple of years and over time had worked at a number of jobs. She enjoyed sales and seemed to be good at it. The irony was that her specialty was engagement and wedding bands. The couples she dealt with were deeply in love and eager to start their lives together. It gave Lauren a deep sense of satisfaction to help them take one of their first steps toward commitment.

The bottom line, she realized now, was that Todd was completely content to leave matters just as they were. They got along great and talked frequently. Rarely a week passed without them attending some sort of social event. They would like to spend more time together, but Todd was busy with his broadcasting career. He had his sights set on getting an anchor position and focused most of his attention on achieving his professional goals.

"Hello, Lauren," Lydia Hoffman said, coming up from behind her.

"Oh, hi." Lauren spun around to greet the owner of the yarn store. Lydia's husband, Brad, had purchased his wife's wedding band at John Michael Jewelers, where Lauren had worked for the past five years.

"Isn't that a beautiful baby blanket?" Lydia asked, apparently noticing Lauren's gaze was focused on the window display.

"It is." Lauren had no option but to agree.

"I think I've sold more yarn from this display than any I've ever done. There's something about knitting for babies that draws people into the shop. Just yesterday a customer stopped by and bought yarn for the blanket and told me she doesn't know anyone who's having a baby, but she thought she'd knit it anyway."

Lauren faked a smile. "I just got word my sister is pregnant." She didn't elaborate and explain that Carol was a full two years younger than she. "When I saw this blanket I thought I should knit it for her."

"I'm sure she'd treasure it. Anything homemade makes a baby gift all the more special."

Lydia inserted the key to the front door, and while Lauren was tempted to purchase the yarn right then, she needed to get to work herself. "I'll be by later today or tomorrow to pick up the yarn."

"Make it Thursday. I'm sold out, but I have a new shipment due in then. I'll be here if you need any help with the pattern," Lydia assured her.

John Michael Jewelers, the high-end jewelry store where Lauren worked, was one block down from the yarn store. Elisa Lippincott, the original owner's daughter, managed the store now with her husband, Garry. Lauren enjoyed her job immensely and considered Elisa a friend as well as her employer.

"Morning," Lauren said as she came into the store. She locked the door behind her. When the safe was open all the doors leading into the store remained locked.

Elisa stuck her head out of the walk-in safe. "Morning," she returned brightly. She had a pair of jewel cases in her hands, which she set into the display window that looked out onto Blossom Street.

Lauren removed her raincoat and stuck it in the back office along with her purse. Right away she helped Elisa get out the precious stones. Despite the down economy the store continued to do well. Elisa, Garry, and Lauren—all working full-time, along with a few part-time sales associates—were a good team.

"Garry will be in sometime this afternoon," Elisa explained as she set out the semiprecious stones. "He's got a meeting at the school for one of the boys, and then he's headed to lunch with the Rotary Club."

Garry was the company expert when it came to men's and women's watches. Lauren headed up their diamond sales, and Elisa handled just about everything else.

"I heard from my sister," Lauren said casually as she set the jewels in the display case, locking them inside. "Carol and Jason are pregnant." She made sure she sounded pleased and excited for her *younger* sibling.

"That's great."

"It is," Lauren agreed. "It's just wonderful. Mom and Dad are over the moon. Their first grandchild."

Elisa paused and focused her attention on Lauren. "You sound like you're ready to cry."

"I could break into sobs at the drop of a pin," she admitted, and tried to laugh it off, but the only sound that came out was reminiscent of something one might hear on the Sci-Fi channel. She quickly got hold of herself. "Tell me, Elisa, and please be honest. Is there something wrong with me?" Because Elisa was her friend, she expected the truth.

"Wrong?"

"Am I annoying?"

"Not at all." Elisa sounded shocked that Lauren would suggest such a thing.

"Do I have a domineering or unpleasant personality?"

"No way."

"Do I bore you?"

"No." Again, her friend shook her head.

"Am I unattractive?"

This question produced a laugh. "Hardly. Have you looked in a mirror lately? You're gorgeous—tall and slim, with your stunning blue eyes and that dark hair. I swear there must be some Scottish blood in you somewhere. Half the men who come in this shop leave half in love with you."

Her friend's words were a balm to her wounded pride. "Then why am I still single?"

Elisa didn't hesitate. "Because Todd Hampton is an idiot." She gently squeezed Lauren's forearm. "You've been much too patient with him. You need to give Todd an ultimatum," she suggested. "He loves you. All he needs now is a gentle shove in the right direction. Tell him it's time; you've been patient to this point, but you aren't willing to continue without a firm commitment."

An ultimatum for Todd—Lauren had reached the same conclusion but then rethought the matter. The fact was she'd spent the majority of the night tossing and turning, mulling over her options with Todd. She'd teetered back and forth with the relationship, wondering what would be best. She hated the idea of forcing him to set a date, and then wondered why she'd been so willing to let matters drag.

"The thing is . . ." Lauren didn't get the opportunity to finish her sentence when Elisa's cell phone chirped.

"It's Katie," Elisa grabbed it before the second chirp.

Lauren knew the shop owner had been anxiously awaiting a call from her oldest child. Katie was a college freshman, and Elisa had undergone separation anxiety sending her only daughter away to school, which was less than three hundred miles away in Pullman, Washington. Elisa worried incessantly over Katie's diet, studies, partying, alcohol, and dating. If Katie didn't contact her mother at some point during the day, Elisa was convinced her child had fallen victim to any number of dreadful possibilities.

"Katie, why haven't you called?" Elisa demanded. "You didn't answer the text message I sent, and—"

Elisa paused, then let out a loud gasp and hurried into the small office, quickly closing the door. Lauren couldn't help but wonder what that was about. Her friend tended to be something of a drama queen. Even with the office door closed, Lauren could hear Elisa, although she couldn't make out what she was saying.

The possibilities raced through Lauren's mind. More than likely, it was something minor. Katie might have flunked an important test. More likely, she needed extra money put into her bank account. Quite possibly, she hadn't turned in her library books on time and allowed the fine to accumulate. Lauren liked Katie and considered the teenager levelheaded and responsible. As a friend and employer, Elisa was great, but as a mother, she was a bit fixated.

Ten minutes later, Elisa reappeared and was as white as a sun-bleached sheet.

"Elisa," Lauren asked tentatively, "is everything all right with Katie?"

Her friend didn't answer and then simply shook her head.

"Do you need to sit down?"

Elisa nodded.

Lauren scooted over a stool, and Elisa sank into it in slow motion.

"Do you want me to call Garry?"

That got an immediate response that came as a shout: "No . . . no!"

"Can I get you coffee?"

"I need something way stronger than coffee. Way stronger."

Lauren didn't think they kept anything more potent at the store, unless it was for a special sales event. Even then it was champagne, and Lauren suspected Elisa wasn't in the mood to celebrate with a glass of bubbly. "Can you tell me what's wrong?"

"I . . . I don't know." Tears welled in Elisa's eyes.

Apparently, this was something far worse than an overdue library book or a failed test. Disregarding what Elisa had claimed she needed, Lauren brewed her a single cup of coffee, making sure it was extra-strong. She added three cubes of sugar and stirred until it had dissolved before delivering it to her friend.

Elisa held on to the cup with both hands as though it was all that was keeping her from falling off the edge of a ten-story building. "Do you remember Dietrich?"

"Of course." Katie had recently brought the farmer's son home during spring break. His family was from the Walla Walla area in the southeast corner of the state. Dietrich's family farm was one of the largest producers of sweet onions in the entire country.

"I didn't like him the minute I met him."

Actually, Elisa had disapproved of the young man

even before she'd met Dietrich. Because he was a senior and three years older than Katie, Elisa was convinced he was too old for her daughter, which was ridiculous. Garry was three years older than Elisa. That was simply an excuse, Lauren suspected, because she didn't want her daughter getting into a serious relationship.

"Did Katie and Dietrich break up?" Lauren asked, although that wouldn't make sense. That news would have relieved Elisa.

"I wish," she snorted. Then, as if realizing she was holding a mug of hot coffee in her hands, she sipped it. After one taste, she grimaced. "I can't believe this is happening. It's a nightmare." Squeezing her eyes shut, she shook her head and then covered her mouth with her hand.

"Katie isn't . . ."

Elisa nodded. "My daughter is pregnant. She's only nineteen. She's a baby herself, and now she insists that she loves Dietrich and wants to marry him. Tell me, Lauren, do you honestly see Katie married . . ."

"Ah . . ." Lauren hardly knew what to say.

"It's ridiculous. Utterly ridiculous. She's far too young."

Lauren sat down next to her friend. "What did you tell her?" Lauren asked concerned. There'd been a lot of shouting going on.

"What else? I insisted she come home immediately. There are ways of dealing with situations like this. I never thought I'd say this, but I can't allow my daughter to go through with this pregnancy. A baby now would ruin her life. We've got to think about her future."

"Isn't this Katie's decision?" Lauren asked gently.

Elisa's eyes snapped with anger. "Not you too."

"Me?"

"That's what Katie said, and she insists she's going to have this baby. She's convinced she's in love with that . . . that farmer."

Now didn't seem a good time to remind Elisa that at age twenty-two Dietrich was an adult and, from what Lauren had seen, a responsible, kindhearted one.

"He took advantage of Katie," Elisa insisted, straightening now.

"Is that what Katie said?"

"Oh, no, she wouldn't admit to anything like that. Instead, she defended him and insisted they were equally responsible."

Personally, Lauren felt this was a matter between Katie and Dietrich and that Elisa would be well advised to let them decide how best to deal with the situation.

"I insisted Katie come home right away, but she refused." Elisa took another taste of the coffee and made a gulping sound as though it was difficult to swallow.

"I wish I knew what to say," Lauren confessed. She felt at a loss and wasn't certain she had anything of value to contribute.

"This is history repeating itself," Elisa whispered, and wiped away a tear that had spilled out from the corner of her eye. "Garry and I . . . I was pregnant at nineteen, too."

Naturally, Lauren realized Elisa and Garry had married young. They must have, in order to have a daughter in college. Identical twin boys followed three years later. Tim and Tom were high school sophomores and played varsity on the high school soccer and baseball teams. Lauren had attended their games with Elisa and Garry. Because of their connection, Todd had done a human-interest story on the boys that played on the local evening news.

"It turned out fine between you and Garry," Lauren reminded Elisa.

"Well, yes, but my family always liked Garry. I agree we were young and foolish. Dad wasn't happy with me—Mom either, for that matter—but Dad took Garry under his wing, taught him the business. Dad saw to it that when it came time for him and Mom to retire, Garry and I were capable of taking over the store." Elisa hung her head. "I can't imagine what my parents will say when they hear about this." Right away she straightened. "They will never know. I'll make sure of that. If Katie won't come to me, then she gives me no other option but to go to her."

Lauren resisted the urge to advise her friend not to act on impulse.

"I'm booking a flight right this minute." With a look of determination, Elisa reached for her cell.

"Do you want me to contact Garry?" Lauren asked.

Elisa looked aghast. "Why would you do that?"

"To cover for you while you're away."

"Oh." Elisa set down her phone and exhaled a long, slow breath. She brushed the hair off her forehead while she thought matters through. "I'd better wait and talk to him about this. I swear if he knew before me I'll shoot the man for keeping it a secret."

"Did Katie tell you how far along she is?" Lauren asked.

"No. When I asked, she refused to answer."

Lauren suspected Katie might have been pregnant when she was in Seattle for spring break last month. No wonder she'd brought Dietrich home with her. Lauren had met the young man only once and had immediately liked him. He was polite and respectful and seemed intelligent. She remembered watching him with Katie and feeling a pinch of envy at the way he couldn't keep his eyes off her.

All at once it hit Lauren. A double whammy. Her younger sister was pregnant, and now her dearest friend, who was only a few years older than Lauren, was about to become a grandmother.

Without weighing the decision, she retrieved her cell and called Todd. Generally, she avoided contacting him during work hours, but he wasn't on the set until right before noon. As best she could figure, he would be sitting in a chair in the makeup room.

He answered on the third ring. "Hey, honey, what's up?" Todd sounded rushed and a bit distracted. She half expected him to remind her that it wasn't good practice to contact him while he was at work.

"Can you meet me tonight?"

"Tonight?" he repeated. "Can't. I'm taping a story for the eleven-o'clock report."

"What about Thursday?" Any night was fine for what she had in mind. Lauren had made her decision.

"Thursday it is," Todd agreed. "Be sure and watch the noon news. And I've got a lead on a great story. I'll tell you about it later. We'll talk more about it on Thursday. Gotta go."

With that, the line was disconnected. It wasn't until she heard the buzz in her ear that she realized she hadn't had time to ask where they should meet or what time.